THE STORY OF THE BEAST

Magister Hickory drew in a deep breath and sat up straight once again. "One of our original members was a wizard named Nettle....In his nightwork he conjured up a Beast from the black side of our souls. Bit by bit, he quilted that Beast together, until it had swallowed up—"

"Excuse me," said Thornmallow, his voice soft with fear, "but I don't understand. I mean—wouldn't it be a good idea to lose the black side?"

Magister Hickory smiled indulgently. "By 'black,' my prickly friend, I do not mean evil. Or wicked. I mean dark and deep, as in the black water of the deepest lakes. All those *strongest of emotions* that—if used improperly— tempt us to wicked, evil deeds....Tonight when the Master comes...he will slowly leach out the rest of our strong emotions, feeding them to his Quilted Beast, making it grow huge with our stolen feelings. If we cannot stop him, he will make us all disappear, and he will then own Wizard's Hall."

Other Books by Jane Yolen

Twelve Impossible Things Before Breakfast

The Young Merlin Trilogy:
Passager
Hobby
Merlin

The Wild Hunt

The Pit Dragon Trilogy:
Dragon's Blood
Heart's Blood
A Sending of Dragons

The Transfigured Hart

Here There Be Dragons
Here There Be Unicorns
Here There Be Witches
Here There Be Angels
Here There Be Ghosts

WIZARD'S HALL

JANE YOLEN

Magic Carpet Books
Harcourt, Inc.
SAN DIEGO   NEW YORK   LONDON

For Bonnie,
who wanted this book from the beginning.
And for Heidi,
who reads them all.

Text copyright © 1991 by Jane Yolen
Illustrations copyright © 1991 by Trina Schart Hyman

First Magic Carpet Books edition 1999
First published 1991

Magic Carpet Books is a registered trademark of Harcourt, Inc.

Library of Congress Cataloging-in-Publication Data
Yolen, Jane.
Wizard's hall/by Jane Yolen.
p.   cm.
"Magic Carpet Books."
Summary: A young apprentice wizard saves the wizard's training hall
by trusting and believing in himself.
[1. Fantasy. 2. Wizards—Fiction. 3. Magic—Fiction.
4. Perseverance (Ethics)—Fiction.] I. Title.
PZ7.Y78Wk 1991
[Fic]—dc20   90-45445
ISBN 0-15-202085-3

Text set in Janson Text.
Designed by Martha Roach
L N O M K
Printed in the United States of America

CONTENTS

PROLOGUE   vii

1. *Our Hero*   1

2. *Into the Hall*   7

3. *Thornmallow Gets to Class*   15

4. *First Spell*   23

5. *Rules*   31

6. *Meeting*   36

7. *Not a Wizard*   45

8. *Classes*   52

Contents

9. Eavesdropping   58

10. Telling Tales   68

11. The Master Speaks   74

12. The Story of the Beast   79

13. Ideas   86

14. Library Time   91

15. Full Moon Night   97

16. The Master and the Beast   102

17. Magister Hickory's Defense   107

18. The End of Wizard's Hall   111

19. Thornmallow Really Tries   115

20. Unquilting the Beast   121

21. Saving Wizard's Hall   125

22. The Enhancer   129

PROLOGUE

Thornmallow was a wizard, only the most minor of wizards. He had learned some elementary Spelling and a smattering of Names. He had not yet learned his Changes thoroughly, nor his Transformations. And his Curses tended to splatter or dribble around the edges. He was rarely Punctual or Practical and his nose tended toward smudginess.

But he meant well. And he tried.

Magister Greybane of the long, thin beard was often heard to mutter when Thornmallow came for lessons in Prestonomics. Magister Beechvale had sick headaches when it was Thornmallow's turn to chant. And even Magister Briar Rose was known to feel a bit queasy upon the occasion of Thornmallow's exams.

But the fact remains that Thornmallow meant well.

And he tried. He came to Wizard's Hall at the time of its greatest peril, the 113th student, the very last to be admitted in that horrible year. And it turned out the inhabitants of Wizard's Hall were glad indeed that Thornmallow studied there.

Not because he was the world's greatest wizard.

But because he meant well.

And he tried.

1

OUR HERO

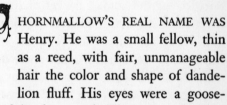HORNMALLOW'S REAL NAME WAS Henry. He was a small fellow, thin as a reed, with fair, unmanageable hair the color and shape of dandelion fluff. His eyes were a gooseberry green and hard to read. There was always a smudge or two on his nose as if the nose led him into trouble. But actually he was a quiet boy, shy and obedient to a fault.

He had never wanted to be a wizard.

As a youngster he'd fancied being a linewalker or a tree warden or a juggler, mostly outside work. But he'd outgrown each fancy in turn, as children often do, moving on to the next with hardly a backward glance.

One day, when he was eleven, he mentioned wizardry to his dear ma. He didn't mean it. Not really. It was just a passing thought.

She looked up from her butter churn and smiled.

"That's the job for you *(Whomp!)*," she said. "Steady work and *(Whomp!)* a good place in the world. That's the one." She gave one last *Whomp!* to the churn, got up from her stool, and with her kerchief wiped a smudge off Henry's nose. Then, stretching to get the knots out of her spine, she walked into the house to help him pack. She was never one for delay. She stuffed the bag with a change of shirts, a pair of woollies for the cold, a packet of rose petals for the sweetening, and hard journeycake for the road.

"That's the one!" she repeated with even more enthusiasm. "You had a great-uncle on your father's side — bless his soul — who took to wizardry." She hesitated, then shook her head. "Or was it card playing? Whatever."

"But what if I have no talent for it, Ma?" Henry had asked, somewhat sensibly and not a little nervous that she was packing him off so quickly.

"Talent don't matter," she'd answered, closing the bag. "I didn't know I had any talent for mothering until you came along. And look!" She gestured to him as if he were proof enough. "It only matters that you try."

Then she kissed him three times, once on each

cheek for love and once on the forehead for wisdom, wiped his smudgy nose one last time, and closed the door behind him saying, "Don't forget to write."

Henry stared at his house for a long minute and bit his lower lip until tears came to his eyes. But he was a good boy and used to doing what he was told. So, wiping his eyes and leaving a brand-new smudge on the right side of his nose, he waved goodbye to his ma. Her smile shone out of the window at him like an off-center crescent moon. Then he turned. He could feel her smile warming his back and her kisses protecting his cheeks and face as he started on the road. Indeed, he didn't know if he had any talent for wizardry. Or for card playing. Whatever.

But he certainly knew he could try.

The way to Wizard's Hall was no secret. It was just over the Far-Rise Hills, turn left until morning. Every child in Hallowdale knew that. There was even a jump-rope rhyme about it:

> Tell me the place where wizards dwell,
> Tell me each step and turning,
> Over the mountains, under the hill,
> Turn left and walk till morning.

That certainly didn't rhyme as well as it might, but it fit the *tip-taps* of a jump rope perfectly. And of course, there ahead of him were the Far-Rise Hills, a day's journey away.

Henry needed no map.

It was late fall, and the last of autumn's colors had faded to a steady rust carpet beneath bare trees. Short bursts of wind hissed and hooted and whistled down the valley, pushing Henry onward from Hallowdale as surely as his dear ma had pushed him out the door.

The walk to the foothills was easy — a smooth and gently turning path lined with trees. Henry dodged a scallywag and two highwaymen along the way, but that was just in case. He doubted they had any interest in his poor goods. The journeycake was crumbled, and the woollies were well worn. But still he hid behind the trees, for his dear ma had always cautioned, *Better take care than need care.*

He also spent an hour up one of the taller beeches when a family of wild boar rooted by. Henry was no hero. Being small and thin had practically guaranteed that. Besides, he'd no practice in the art of being brave. To make up the time lost shivering amongst the leaves, he forwent both lunch and dinner until he was within sight of the hills.

"And isn't it a marvel," he whispered to himself as he chewed the crumbly cake, "just how good a dry meal can be. No wonder my dear ma always says, *Hunger is a great seasoner.*"

At the mountain's foot was a sign to make the passage simpler still:

THIS WAY TO WIZARD'S HALL

it announced in bold lettering. There was also a gold-leafed arrow, picked a bit raw by passing villains, pointing to the left. And sure enough, the path continued right up the mountain's face, with little yellow ribands marking every fifth tree, just as a reminder.

Clearly no one could get lost along the way.

Henry walked all night long. His only companions were the owls who swooped silently above him, for the crickets and frogs were long gone to their early winterings. Henry was actually glad of the quiet.

In the morning both sun and moon shone together, and right below them Henry could make out the towers of Wizard's Hall, standing tall and jagged against the sky. He knew there would be gardens, rosebushes, and trees. Everyone knew magic made things grow. Like manure. But the towers reminded Henry of the teeth of a great beast, and suddenly he was quite sure he didn't want to study wizardry at all. He knew with certainty that he'd make a better farmer or fisherman or even a cook.

He tried to turn and go home.

But as if the road itself knew it was Henry's fate to go to Wizard's Hall, it wouldn't let him turn. No sooner did he lift one foot to go home than the other was stuck fast. He could only move forward toward the Hall, not back.

It was magic for sure — and he was part of it.

He ran his tired fingers through his hair and remembered his ma's smile at the window. He remembered some of her last words.

"It only matters that you try."

Shrugging the pack higher on his shoulders, he sighed once out loud and thought he heard an answering sigh in the wind.

"To Wizard's Hall, then," he whispered.

The road loosed both his feet at once and tumbled him forward at a run toward his new home.

2

INTO THE HALL

IZARD'S HALL WAS A SOLIDLY BUILT place of jagged stone towers and long arching windows. High gray stone walls curved around it, set with ironwork gates. There was not a tree or plant growing within the boundaries of those walls; it was as if magic had shattered the natural world.

Henry shivered when he looked through the gates and saw how barren the yard was, for he had been expecting much green. But he knew he could not fight his fate. So he walked steadily till he reached the main gate. There the iron was twisted into intricate symbols of power, laid out in a grid that looked like a quilt or like a beast — depending upon which eye he squinted with. It made his stomach queasy just looking.

Taking a deep breath, Henry knocked upon the gate and called out, "Hallooo?"

The gate made a rude sound, remarkably like a spit kazoo, and a small door just Henry's size opened in it.

Henry let out the breath he'd been holding. Red-faced, he trudged in.

Suddenly he found himself not in the barren yard nor yet in a hallway, but in a wood-paneled room hung with gray-blue tapestries fraying a bit at the sides. A large table, littered with parchment, stood in the center of the room. Some pieces of parchment were rolled up tightly with scarlet ribands, some were creased and folded, some were scrunched and discarded, some were held flat by dark inkwells or brass doorknobs or apple cores.

Behind the table sat an old man with skin the color of the parchment, eyes like blue marbles, and a white halo of hair.

"Good evening," the old man said gently.

As it was not evening at all but midday, and sunlight streamed in through the many-paned windows, quilting the floor with light, Henry was stuck for an answer.

"Or good morning," the old man added. "Which-

8

ever. I am Register Oakbend. Glad to meet you at last."

"At last?" Henry said. "But nobody knew I was coming. Not even me. Till yesterday."

The old man did not reply to this but merely held out his hand.

Only then did Henry realize that the wizard was quite blind, for his marble-blue eyes stared straight ahead and his hand was reaching slightly to the left of the table, though Henry was slightly to the right.

"Actually, sir," Henry said, gathering his courage, "it's coming on to noon."

Register Oakbend turned at Henry's voice so that now he was facing Henry directly, and lowered his hand. "I *said* whichever," he answered peevishly. "And that includes noon, young man. What did you say your name was?"

"Henry," said Henry, "though I didn't actually say it — yet."

"Said it now," said Register Oakbend. "The Book says *Better now than not*. But isn't Henry a silly name? H-E-N-R-Y, don't you know. Or H-E-N-R-I-E. Nothing to it. Simply a series of sounds without meaning. HEN-ER-REE. Now *Couchwillow*, there's a good one. Or *Stickybun*. Or *Daffy-down-dilly*, though that's really for a girl. How about *Broadleaf*? Do you like it? Does it fit?"

"Please, sir," said Henry in a quiet little voice, "my name is Henry."

"Listen carefully, boy. Words mean something, not just sounds thrown down willy-nilly. *Willy-nilly* — that's not a bad one. But I didn't ask what your name *is*. We haven't decided that yet. And you're going to need a good one. I asked what your name *was*." He cocked his head to one side.

"But, sir, my name has always been Henry. Always will be. My dear ma gave it to me." Henry's voice quavered a little bit at the mention of her.

"Despite popular opinion," Register Oakbend said, "mothers do not always know best. Especially about names. That is why children get called so many other things by their friends. I, for example, was called Niddy-Noddy by my companions, though my name at the time was Ned." He smiled, remembering.

"But my dear ma —" Henry began.

"Prickly sort of fellow, isn't he," murmured Register Oakbend. "But just what we desperately need."

Henry thought the old man was talking to himself until he heard an answering sound.

"*Squark!*" It came from a little white animal in a cage that was almost obscured by the mounds of parchment. Henry caught just a glimpse of it.

"Absolutely," replied Register Oakbend, nodding his head vigorously. "Right idea. That's the ticket."

"Squark?" Henry asked.

"Your name," the old man said. "Your name for *is*; for *now*; for Wizard's Hall."

"Squark," Henry repeated dismally, thinking for a moment about running away. Only for a moment. He was, after all, a good boy. And he *had* promised he would try. "Squark."

"Means Thornmallow: prickly on the outside, squishy within. Though I'll have to take that *squishy* on faith. But Dr. Mo is always right."

"Thornmallow," Henry whispered to himself, trying it out. Oddly he felt relieved. Thornmallow was certainly a great deal better than Squark for a name. And it was only his name for *is*, for *now*, for Wizard's Hall. When he went home for holidays, he could still be Henry to his dear ma. Closing his eyes for a moment, he tried to feel like Thornmallow the Wizard. He only felt like Henry, thin as a reed with a nose that was often smudgy. Suddenly he remembered something and opened his eyes.

"Who is Dr. Mo?" he asked.

But Register Oakbend, cage, desk, and all had unaccountably disappeared.

Henry — now Thornmallow — croggled, swallowed hard, and looked around. He was no longer inside the Hall but outside it, this time in the treeless, shrubless, flowerless yard, standing on hard cobbles. Not sure what it all meant, he walked up to the front door. It, like the gate, was covered with a grid, but this grid looked entirely like a quilt and not at all like a beast. That made him feel a bit better. He knocked on it.

The door made a sighing noise and opened. Thornmallow walked in.

He was quite surprised that now it was cozy and snug inside, not unlike a larger version of his cottage. Unaccountably, he felt at home. Small gold-framed portraits of wizards hung along one wall, each of them looking old and wise. Beneath each frame was a name.

"Magister Greybane," he read silently. "Magister Bledwort. Magister Hyssop. Magister Briar Rose." Something about the last wizard reminded Henry of his dear ma. Perhaps it was because she was the only one smiling. He said her name aloud: "Magister Briar Rose."

The picture winked at him.

"I must be tired," Henry told himself and suddenly recalled he'd been walking all night. But when the picture winked a second time, mouthing his name, he felt his knees give way, and he sat down quite suddenly on the polished floor.

"Now, now, none of that, child," came a small voice from the picture. "It won't do. You are the last, and what we desperately need, and therefore most important to us. Be strong and stand. You must try, dear child. You *must* try."

The voice was remarkably like his dear ma's, only older. Henry stood at once, not even bothering to

12

wonder what being *the last* meant or how desperate they were at Wizard's Hall.

Addressing the picture, he said, "Pardon me, Madame Magister, but my name is Hen — er — Thornmallow. I'm not quite sure what's happening, but I've come to try and be a wizard."

"Well, of course you have, Thornmallow," the picture answered. "Otherwise Door wouldn't have let you in, and Dr. Mo wouldn't have given you a name. You'd still be outside and called Hen-er. Now you are inside and called Thornmallow. Hmmmmmm, Thornmallow. Prickly on the outside, squishy within. I'll have to take that *prickly* on faith. But prickly is just what we need. Let's get you settled, shall we? And wipe that smudge off your nose."

Suddenly a small, compact woman in a musty, wine-colored robe with something that could have been egg stains on the front, stood by his side. The picture frame was empty. She plucked a handkerchief from the air and scrubbed at his face with it. Then, apparently satisfied, she guided him with two fingers on his elbow into a small room immediately to the right.

"This will be yours," she said. "See?" She made a quick gesture with her hand, and the handkerchief disappeared. At the same time, a portrait of his dear ma with her butter churn appeared on a small wooden stand. His clothes, clean-smelling and ironed, winkled out of his pack and hung themselves on pegs by the door. A little quilt covered with sunbursts tucked itself tidily over the bed.

"Do you like it?" asked Magister Briar Rose.

Thornmallow picked up the picture from the stand and collapsed onto the bed. He was about to thank Magister Briar Rose when he saw that in the picture his dear ma seemed quite sad.

Bursting into sobs, Thornmallow put his face into his hands and was quite a long time at it. When he was quiet at last, he looked up, but the wizard was gone.

"All this appearing and disappearing," Thornmallow told himself between sniffles, wishing the handkerchief hadn't vanished as well, "can be awfully hard on a body." At his words a handkerchief dropped out of the air, landing beside him on the bed.

NOW BLOW, in little flaming letters, flashed above the handkerchief.

He blew until his nose was quite clear. Then he lay down on the bed with the picture of his dear ma pressed next to his heart. He was asleep at once.

3

THORNMALLOW
GETS TO CLASS

HEN THORNMALLOW AWOKE, HE felt refreshed. Opening his eyes, he blinked twice, not quite believing what he saw. On the ceiling of his room was a star map with little lights that winked off and on, reciting their own names.

"The Ram," one group of stars said. "The Hunter," whispered another.

He sat up.

Someone had taken off his boots and tucked them side by side under his bed. He reached over, picked them up, and drew them back on. They were freshly polished. He could almost see his face in them. Sitting on his bed, he began to wonder if all the magicks he had seen were tricks — or real.

15

Real! he decided at last and stood.

"The Bear," answered the stars.

When he opened the door of his room, he saw a long hall. Out of many similar doors poured boys his own age. Some were tall, some short, some weighty, and some as slim as he. None of them seemed to have combed their hair, though one — a boy with a bright yellow cock's comb — was intent on slicking his hair back with hasty fingers. All the boys were wearing long black scholastic gowns and carrying books.

"New boy?" called one as he raced by, going right to left. He was tall, with flaming red hair and a network of freckles like a map over his nose and cheeks.

Before Thornmallow could answer, the boy and his companions were gone. Not disappeared this time, but gone around a corner of the building. Thornmallow hurried after them and found himself in another long hall, this one filled with rushing girls in black scholar's robes running toward the right.

"Last bell!" one girl cried. She had a face the color of old wood, and her black hair was caught up in three plaits of equal weight: one on each side of her head and one standing straight up from it. She was short, with the eager look of certain small dogs.

"What bell?" Thornmallow ventured, but his words were immediately drowned out by three enormous and quite unmelodious *bong*s.

Even as the third *bong* sounded, the girls disappeared, funneling into separate rooms.

Standing in the middle of the now-empty hall, Thornmallow stared about him. His gooseberry eyes were wide, and his heart skiproped in his chest.

"What next?" he whispered. Being a wizard had so far been full of rushings about, of comings and goings, appearances and disappearances, not at all what he'd expected. But — as his dear ma was fond of saying — *Expectations always disappoint.*

Something touched his elbow. He jumped and turned to see Magister Briar Rose. There was something rather like strawberry jam on her right sleeve.

"About your classes," she said. "Close your eyes."

He obeyed. When she told him to open his eyes again, they were in another room, this one filled floor-to-ceiling with books. Or at least he and Magister Briar Rose were in the room. His stomach, he was sure, had been left behind.

"Don't worry," the old woman said. "You'll soon get used to it. Sit!"

He did as she commanded, collapsing onto the floor.

"Wherever did you learn your manners?" Magister Briar Rose asked. "Sit in the chair." She pointed. "Over there." She sat herself behind a book-littered table and poured herself a cup of black tea. Then she snatched a cracker from a nearby basket.

17

Red-faced, Thornmallow stood and walked over to the perfectly respectable high-backed wooden chair she had pointed at and lowered himself carefully onto its plump purple cushion.

There was a long silence while she seemed to be examining Thornmallow and the cracker alternately and with equal attention.

"Please, ma'am," he said at last, "may I ask a question?"

"Of course," she said. "But just the one. We have a great deal of business to get on with, now that you are finally here." As she spoke, she dipped the cracker into the tea.

"Then, ma'am, what is a *magister?*"

"Why — a teacher," she said and took a small bite of the now soggy cracker.

"Then . . ." He paused a minute, screwing up his courage, as he wasn't sure if this was a second question he was asking or part of the first.

"Then what, child? We haven't got all day." She brushed cracker crumbs off her chest.

"Then . . . why not just say *teacher?*"

"Ah." She leaned back and smiled at him, and he knew it was all right. "There's nothing magical about the word *teacher*, is there? Everyone knows it, and therefore it's common and not fraught with magic. And we are about the business of magic here. There

18

is this to remember: magic is tough and sometimes dangerous, and the words you use are always important."

Thornmallow was not sure he understood it all, but as she did not seem to want to elaborate, he had to be content. He was sure she would not tolerate another question.

"Now next time," Briar Rose said, "you must wear a scholar's robe."

He nodded, not even daring to ask where such a robe might be found.

"Why, in the wardrobe of course," she answered as if he had spoken aloud. "And now to your studies." She put the half-eaten cracker down. It jumped back into the basket.

Thornmallow gulped.

"Can you spell?"

Catching his breath, Thornmallow said in a voice that sounded rather as if it had suddenly ripped on a nail, "C-A-T spells *cat?*"

Magister Briar Rose chuckled, but it was not meant meanly at all. In fact it sounded as if she were laughing at herself instead of at Thornmallow. "No, child, not that kind of spelling. This kind. C-A-T . . ." She waved her hand in a decidedly odd manner and pointed at the floor.

A calico cat, hardly more than a kitten, materialized. It looked up with but a moment's surprise in its green eyes, then settled at once into cleaning its back leg, ignoring them both.

"No," Thornmallow whispered. "Not at all like that."

The cat stopped cleaning itself, stood, and stalked out of the room.

"Elementary Spelling, then," Magister Briar Rose said, nodding her head and making a note of it on a piece of parchment. "What about Names?"

"Thornmallow," Thornmallow whispered. "Or Henry."

"Andrew-John-Bruce-David-Bob," intoned Magister Briar Rose, staring at him.

Thornmallow felt himself growing smaller and smaller and smaller still—until he sat at the edge of a vast purple meadow that seemed to stretch behind him forever.

"No names," he said, his voice as tiny as he.

"Bob-Divad-Ecurb-Nhoj-Werdna," came a booming from above him. Magister Briar Rose was reciting the names backward.

Slowly Thornmallow expanded, as if he were steadily being pumped full of air. When the names stopped, he was his right size again.

"First Year Names, then," Magister Briar Rose added to her list, "though I thought that your arrival heralded something more exacting than that. How you can possibly help as a First Year is beyond me." She shrugged and cocked her head to one side. "Any Transformations?"

"None — none at all," Thornmallow squeaked quickly.

"Ah. Ah," she agreed. "I didn't expect so. Though I did hope . . ." A third line was added to the growing list. "Curses?"

He shook his head, afraid to make a sound.

She scratched the last of it onto the parchment and signed her name on the bottom with a flourish that, especially upside-down, looked nothing like Briar Rose. Then she dropped a bit of red wax onto the parchment from a burning taper and took a great seal shaped rather like the handle of a butter churn. With it she set her mark into the wax.

Just then, the room went dark, the light blinking off and leaving Thornmallow with an awful feeling, as if pins and needles were sticking all over his body. A moment later the lights went on again.

"Was that a Curse, ma'am?" he asked. "Or a Transformation?"

Magister Briar Rose had an odd look on her face, and there were white spots on her cheek. *"That,"* she said finally, "is a failure of power. You do not need to know more." She took a deep breath. "And *this* is for you." She handed him the list. "Now you are ready. And I hope — I truly hope — that you will do."

"Do what?" he began to ask, but the moment his hand touched the parchment, he found himself in a classroom. An elderly gentleman with thick drooping mustaches tied over his chest in a gray bow was sitting at the front on a high stool. He looked like some kind of long-legged bird on a nest. Before him, at small, compact desks, twenty boys and girls were chanting a rhyme.

Thornmallow no longer marveled at how he had gotten there. He only wondered if his stomach would ever catch up.

4

FIRST SPELL

HORNMALLOW, IS IT?" ASKED THE gentleman with the mustaches. His voice was harsh and storklike. "Here at last to answer our need. Are you prickly on the outside?"

"Not really, sir," Thornmallow answered.

The man looked at him very sternly for a moment more, then checked something off on a paper that had suddenly materialized in his hand. "Yes, definitely prickly, I'd say, though I shall have to take that inside *squishy* on faith." He crumpled the paper, and it flared with a blue light and disappeared. "I am Magister Beechvale. Fifth row, fourth seat, if you please."

Thornmallow looked at the fifth row, fourth seat. It was occupied.

23

"Sir — " he began.

"Between Tansy and Willoweed. They will keep an eye on you these first days. First days are always difficult." He lifted his hand in a languid manner, as if pointing to the row, but his fingers wiggled mysteriously.

Thornmallow looked again. An empty school desk now stood ahead of the final desk. It was the fourth seat in the fifth row.

"Well — go ahead, boy," Magister Beechvale said in his stork voice.

Thornmallow walked to the desk and stared at it for a minute.

"Sit!" came the teacher's command.

He sat.

"Told you it was last bell," whispered the girl in the desk just ahead of his. She turned as she spoke and smiled at him. Her three black plaits seemed to wave a greeting.

Tansy, Thornmallow thought. *How odd. Tansy is a bright yellow flower, and she is a dark brown girl. If names are supposed to mean something, why isn't she called Bark or Earth.*

Someone tapped him on the shoulder. When he looked, he saw it was the redheaded boy with the freckle map on his face.

"Well come to Wizard's Hall, Thornmallow," he

24

said, "and welcome as well. I'm Willoweed. Your expert guide. *Guardians*, we call them."

Thornmallow nodded. "Hello, Willoweed."

"We just call him Will," Tansy said. "And I am your other guardian. Everyone gets two guardians the first days. That's because first days are — "

"Always difficult," Will cut in.

Thornmallow was about to explain that his real name was not Thornmallow at all, and they could call him Henry, when the sharp clearing of a throat made him look up. Standing on his long bird legs, Magister Beechvale was pointing to the blackboard with a thin wand. Three words glowed at the tip:

PUNCTUALITY!
PRACTICALITY!
PERSONALITY!

The wand tapped three times, and all the students recited as one. "Punctuality! Practicality! Personality!" Their voices were bell-like.

Thornmallow thought he'd better join in, and by the second round he'd added his voice to theirs, but somehow he was a whole tone off.

Someone in a nearby seat giggled. Thornmallow closed his mouth.

"Clear, round, perfect tones if you please," called

out Magister Beechvale, "on these three important beginning words of wizardly wisdom." He hummed a note, and the class hummed after him. They began again on the first word.

Thornmallow tried once more. This time he was off by a tone and a half.

A blond girl in the front row raised her hand.

Magister Beechvale lifted the wand from the board. "Yes, Gorse?"

"Please, sir, but the new boy is tone-deaf."

"Nonsense!" Magister Beechvale replied. "No one admitted to Wizard's Hall is tone-deaf. Dr. Mo would sense it right away and send him packing. A wizard cannot be tone-deaf. And why is that, class?"

Together they sang, "A spell must be chanted on the dominant, or it will fail."

Thornmallow rose reluctantly to his feet. He had no idea what a dominant was, but he did know something else. "Please, sir, if you mean by tone-deaf that I cannot sing on key, well I am afraid that Mistress — er — Gorse is right. My dear ma always said, *Can't carry a tune in a brass bucket!* And on holidays old Master Robyn, the choirmaster, always cautioned me to just mouth the words when we sang the hymns. Tone-deaf — that's me!"

"Nonsense!" Magister Beechvale said again, only this time he sounded more like a screech owl than a stork. His mustaches waggled furiously. "You are just not trying hard enough. Sit down, young Thorn-apple."

"Thorn*mallow*, sir," Thornmallow whispered.

"Prickly indeed," muttered the magister, raising his stick to the board once more. "And we don't encourage *prickly* in my class. See to it you do not answer back again."

Thornmallow sat down and mouthed the rest of the recitation without a sound while the others sang joyfully around him. Hearing no rough edges on the notes, Magister Beechvale actually smiled.

Eventually they moved on from the wizard's wisdoms to a spell about roses in the snow, then one about dresses made of paper, and finally one about letting milk down from a dry cow. Thornmallow thought that the last might be something his dear ma could use. But this time, when he tried to join the chanting, he was at least two full tones wrong, and everyone in row four turned round to stare at him.

"To the front!" Magister Beechvale called three times.

At first Thornmallow didn't think the call was meant for him. Next he tried to *pretend* it wasn't for him. But the third time Magister Beechvale summoned, he added a couple of finger waggles, and without meaning to, Thornmallow leaped from his seat and trotted up to the front of the room. When, at

Magister Beechvale's request, he turned and faced the other boys and girls, twenty pairs of eyes were staring at him, coldly waiting.

"You will sing each note with me," Magister Beechvale said, putting his hands over Thornmallow's ears. "And this time, you must really try." He hummed a note.

Thornmallow closed his eyes and thought for a moment about his dear ma. He *would,* he really *would* try. When he opened them again, though he couldn't actually *hear* the note Magister Beechvale was humming, the teacher's hands being clean over his ears, something else was happening. It was as if a quiet heat were radiating from those hands, spreading around and then into his ears, like some sort of little animal finding its wintering in a cave. The heat sought out the twisting tunnels of his ears and burrowed right down into his brain. And when it hit his brain, a tone sprang into it. He opened his mouth, and the heat — and the tone — came out.

The first note was not nearly close enough, but the second warm note was closer. By the third, he was right smack on pitch, and all the students applauded.

"I can feel it!" he cried out. "I can feel the note." It seemed to be going directly from Magister Beechvale's hands into his ears and out his mouth.

He was so excited, he called out the first spell they'd tried, surprised that he remembered it:

Red against white,
Day into night,
Let the winds blow,
Roses in snow.

It was so wonderful to sing in tune and to remember without trying that Thornmallow waved his hand in time to the chant. Only when Magister Beechvale's hands suddenly slipped off his ears, and he heard the sharp intake of breath from the class, did Thornmallow realize that something had gone wrong.

"Oooooh, the new boy's gonna get it!" cried blond Gorse, staring at the window.

Everyone followed her gaze, and then Thornmallow heard the *thud-thud-thud* as twenty bodies hit the floor and hid under their desks.

That sound was quickly swallowed up by another, louder noise as the windows all snapped open. The sky turned black. And an avalanche of snow bore down on the classroom, caving in the wall and covering Magister Beechvale and his stool.

On top of the snowdrift, which was almost as high as the ceiling, and right above the spot where the stool had been buried, sat a rosebush in full bloom, its petals drifting down like bloodspots against the white snow.

"Perhaps," Magister Beechvale said as he emerged from the drift, "perhaps . . ." His voice was suddenly soft and not at all storklike. He hesitated, dusting off great gobs of snow from his black robe. "Perhaps you needn't try *quite* so hard, Thornmarrow."

"*Mallow*, sir," Thornmallow whispered, swallowing hard. There were tears in his eyes, and he wanted to explain that he hadn't actually meant an avalanche, hadn't meant to ruin the classroom wall, hadn't meant to scare anyone, certainly hadn't meant to get Magister Beechvale wet. But no words came out, only a weak and embarrassing moan.

With a wave of his hand, Magister Beechvale muttered something under his breath. Immediately the snow disappeared inch by inch, until all that was left was a large damp stain on the floor. The wall rebuilt itself. And the rosebush became potted in a green stone urn with bright pink flamingos painted on the side.

Magister Beechvale gave Thornmallow a careful, quick pat on the head. This time there was no heat emanating from his hand. "Squishy indeed, Thornmallow," he said. "Squishy indeed."

5

RULES

DIDN'T MEAN THAT TO HAPPEN," Thornmallow said when the students were all seated in the dining commons. Tansy sat on one side of him, and Will sat facing him across the table. As they explained it, "Guardians stick tight, like cockleburs to clothes."

"I didn't mean all the snow to come and break down the wall and . . ." He suddenly ran out of words and stared glumly into the bowl in front of him. It was full of an earthy brown soup. Cautiously he stuck his spoon in and took a taste. It tasted brown.

"My da says nothing happens by accident," said Gorse, who was sitting on the other side of him. "And he'd know. He's a bush wizard. Of course you meant it."

"Didn't," Thornmallow said, all his sorrow and embarrassment packed into the one word.

"Did."

"Didn't!" he repeated stubbornly.

"Did!" Gorse made a face at her soup.

"What Gorse means," Tansy interrupted, "is that magic can't happen unless it's meant. *Really* meant."

"It's a rule," added Will.

"Rule number five," Gorse said, taking a taste of her own soup and shuddering. "Lizard soup again."

"Lizard?" Thornmallow gulped and put down his spoon.

"Don't pay any attention to old Gooey," Will advised. "She likes to be disgusting. I have ten sisters just like her. Ignoring them works wonders."

"*Lizard*," Thornmallow whispered hopelessly, staring down into the brown soup.

"Only if you want it to be," Tansy said brightly, shaking her finger over his bowl. "See!"

He dared another look. The soup was now bright green, the color of pond scum. That didn't make it any more inviting. He put his spoon in again and brought it slowly to his mouth. The soup still tasted brown.

"I don't understand."

"Well, what did you expect?" Gorse asked. "She's only a first-year student, after all."

"What Gorse means," Will explained, "is that first-year students only learn how to change the face of a thing, not the thing itself. And don't snap, Gooey. We're meant to *help* him."

Gorse stared at Will. "I can snap if I want to, Sillyweed. I'm not his guardian — you are. I was *yours*, because I beat you to Wizard's Hall by a week. That was enough." She turned to Thornmallow. "*Changing the face but not the race.* Rule number one."

Ignoring Gorse, Will said, "For example, if you wanted to add meat to your soup, you could make it appear as if there were meat there."

"We learn to really change one part of a thing at a time in second year," added Tansy.

Will nodded. "In second year, you could change one part of the soup to be meat and it *would* be meat, not just its appearance."

Stirring her spoon in the soup, Gorse said in sepulchral tones, "Taste like meat, smell like meat, feel like meat."

"It would *be* meat," Will continued. "But you couldn't do vegetables. Not at the same time. You can only change one part, you see. The rest of the soup would still be — "

"Brown?" asked Thornmallow.

"You've got it!" Tansy said. "But by third year, you'll know how to change the entire thing."

"You mean, then it could be meat *and* vegetable soup?" asked Thornmallow, so excited he put a hand on Gorse's shoulder and stared eagerly across at Will.

"Lizard!" said Gorse, poking at a lizard that was doing a creditable backstroke across the green liquid in her bowl.

Tansy and Will stared openmouthed at it. "How could he . . . how could it . . . ." Their words dribbled off.

"Well, what happens . . . ," Thornmallow asked withdrawing his hand. The lizard dove expertly to the bottom of the bowl and Will and Tansy both relaxed. "What happens in fourth year?"

"We graduate," said Will.

"Graduate to what?"

"To roast beef!" Gorse replied, in such hopeful tones that Tansy and Will laughed out loud.

"It's a matter of balance," Tansy said. "Magic is all about keeping a balance. Big with little, dark with light, up with down, soft with loud."

"Lizard with roast beef," Gorse added.

They laughed again, and this time even Thornmallow joined in. But as suddenly as he started, he stopped.

"I don't understand at all," he said. "If I am a first-year student and we can only change the face of

34

a thing, not the thing itself, how come I was able to call in all that snow and . . ."

"And break down the wall . . . ," said Will.

"And leave a potted plant," added Tansy.

"And a stain," Thornmallow ended miserably.

"How indeed?" asked Gorse.

No one remarked upon the lizard, for it had not resurfaced, and the soup was once again brown.

The four of them looked at one another for a long moment, the heat of all those questions in their mouths. Then the changing bell shattered the silence and they rose. Whatever answers they might have had were lost in the bell's thunderous voice.

6

MEETING

HEY RAN OUT INTO THE HALLWAY, Will dragging Thornmallow by the arm.

"What . . . ?" Thornmallow began. "Where . . . ?"

"Just follow me," Will said. "I am your guardian. Do what I say."

They were suddenly part of a sea of students surging along the corridor toward a pair of large wooden doors. The solid babble of voices around them drowned out the rest of Thornmallow's questions as he obediently followed Will, but it could not drown out his thoughts.

How could I, a tendril of thought snaked into his brain, *a first-year student with only half a class behind me, have done what I did? Perhaps I have a talent for wizardry after all. Perhaps . . .* and here his thoughts took on the character of a whisper . . . *perhaps I am destined to be a great wizard, even the greatest wizard the Hall has ever known. And won't my dear ma be proud.*

He was grinning broadly by the time Gorse shoved him in the small of the back, and he stumbled forward onto one knee at the foot of a steeply winding iron stairway.

"Up!" Will ordered.

Thornmallow wasn't sure if Will meant him to *get* up or to *go* up. But when Tansy pulled him from in front and Will and Gorse pushed him from behind, he realized that *up* was exactly what Will meant. He got to his feet and began climbing the stairs, though his knee now hurt dreadfully. At the top of the stairs was a balcony overlooking a great meeting room. Gorse shoved him onto one of the many benches, next to a railing. When he put his elbows on the railing and leaned over cautiously, he could see the whole of the room.

It was the largest single room he'd ever been in, bigger even than his dear ma's barn. At the far end was a rounded apse with a speaker's platform below a vaulted ceiling. Behind the platform were three windows made of colored glass pictures. The window on the left showed a wizard in a scholar's robe; the one on the right, a great winged serpent curled around a globe; and in the center was a staff topped by a golden orb with a series of words on a riband banner beneath. Thornmallow was too nearsighted to read the words.

The room quickly filled with students, who scrambled for seats on the benches.

"Upper classes," whispered Tansy. "First year always gets the balcony."

Then a second bell rang. After that, a mighty silence descended upon the students, and Thornmallow found he was holding his breath. Just when he thought he might burst, there was a fanfare of trumpets, and the magisters marched in.

There were thirteen of them in all, dressed in black robes relieved only by long, colorful scarves around their necks. In the lead was a handsome man with a great shag of shoulder-length red-gold hair rather like a lion's mane. He carried a staff topped by an ochreous ball that emitted a yellow light on and off. More on than off.

Thornmallow recognized the staff. "It's the same as in the window. . ."

Will elbowed him in the ribs.

"Shhhh!" Tansy cautioned from the other side.

The line of magisters walked solemnly to the front benches and sat. Thornmallow recognized Magister Beechvale, who was the tallest, his gray mustaches almost hidden by a red-and-blue-striped scarf. And surely the small woman with the purple-and-white scarf near the end was Briar Rose. Bringing up the rear, the one carrying the cage, who felt around the bench with his right hand, had to be Register Oakbend. The rest he didn't recognize.

When all the magisters were seated, the lion-maned leader stood and climbed the three steps up to the platform. Marching to the podium, he set the staff to one side. It hovered several inches above the ground, the light now burning steadily.

"Hail, fellow enchanters," he said.

"Hail, Magister Hickory," they replied.

Thornmallow marveled at how the sound seemed to grow and grow and grow until it filled the entire room, though no more than those few words were spoken.

Then Magister Hickory held up his hand. As if cut by a great knife, the sound abruptly ended. Except for a deep sigh.

Embarrassed, Thornmallow realized that he was the source of that sigh. He put his hand up over his mouth and leaned away from the railing, hoping no one had heard.

Evidently no one had, for Magister Hickory began to speak. His voice was strong and melodic. Thornmallow not only heard the words; he felt them, as if they'd entered his body somewhere below the breast-bone and stayed vibrating there. He leaned forward again.

"Wizard's Hall," said Magister Hickory, "is now full. As of yesterday morning, the one-hundred-and-thirteenth student has entered our doors, taking his place among us." He muttered something under his breath that might have been "At last."

"Aaaah," came the response.

Tansy squeezed Thornmallow's arm. "That's you!" she whispered. "Number one-thirteen. Isn't it wandy?"

"What's *wandy?*" asked Thornmallow.

"Shhhhh!" said Gorse.

Thornmallow bit his lip and was silent.

"But as we all know," Magister Hickory went on, "it says in the *Book of Spells: To begin is not to finish.*"

TO BEGIN IS NOT TO FINISH. The words flashed above Magister Hickory's head, and all around Thornmallow the first-year students nodded in response.

"Look to your right!" ordered Magister Hickory.

Thornmallow jerked to his right and stared. There was Will, and beyond him a boy with yellow hair that curled up and into his ears, and beyond him a boy with a strange green streak in his hair.

"Now look to your left."

Obediently Thornmallow turned to the left. Next

to him was Tansy and beyond her Gorse, and then a skinny boy sticking a finger into his ear.

"Now listen!"

Thornmallow jumped at the thunderous words and focused back on Magister Hickory standing at the rostrum.

"To begin is not to finish." The words behind the magister now flickered a warning red. "Not everyone you have just glanced at will graduate from Wizard's Hall. The course is long. The classes are hard. Some will drop out and become hedge wizards or village herbwives or mere card players in a traveling show. Yet to fail here at the Hall is not to fail in life, only to fail at total deep wizardry." Magister Hickory paused and looked meaningfully around the room. "You would not be here if you did not have talent. Dr. Mo would not allow it."

A strange squeal from the front row came as if in answer, and Magister Hickory smiled down in that direction.

"Yes, yes, Dr. Mo," Magister Hickory said, "you are correct, of course. Talent is not enough."

Behind the rostrum the letters shifted from red to a fierce icy blue. The words TALENT IS NOT ENOUGH glowed at them.

"There is something more you must do, and that something more is — "

"You must try!" Thornmallow cried out the words before he realized what he was doing.

Tansy slapped her hand over his mouth, and Will's hand slammed on top of hers. Gorse hissed a frantic warning. But Magister Hickory had heard this time. He glared up at the balcony, his gaze as icy as the flashing words.

Swiveling in their seats, the upperclassmen searched for the culprit above them, and one by one the magisters, too, turned to stare. All, that is, but Register Oakbend, who sat unmoving, although an excited chittering came from the cage by his side.

"WHO SAID THAT?" roared Magister Hickory.

Slowly Thornmallow disengaged Tansy's and Will's hands from his mouth and stood. They were his guardians but not his guards. If Magister Hickory wanted to know, Thornmallow would have to tell him. It was the only decent, the only right, the only proper thing to do. He wondered briefly what his dear ma would say when he returned in the morning. Surely, talent or no, he was about to be expelled.

"I did, sir."

"WHAT IS YOUR NAME?" Each word Magister Hickory spoke was an arrow below Thornmallow's ribs.

Thornmallow gulped. He wished he could just disappear through the floorboards, out the door, over the Far-Rise Hills, and be home. "Henry, sir."

Dr. Mo squeaked loudly. "*Squark!*" It echoed around the room.

Tansy yanked on his sleeve.

"I mean, Thornmallow, sir," he amended. Then, as if to make up for the awful mistake, he added, "Number one hundred and thirteen, sir."

The hall was hushed. Magister Hickory's eyes bore right into him.

"Ah. So you are number one hundred and thirteen."

"Yes, sir."

"Thornmallow." There was such power behind the name when spoken by Magister Hickory that Thornmallow's knees began to buckle. Will put his hand out to steady him.

"Yes, sir."

"Repeat what you just shouted out, Thornmallow."

Thornmallow drew in a deep breath, so deep he felt light-headed. "*You must try,*" he said, surprised his voice wasn't quaking. His knees certainly were.

There was a long moment of the deepest silence. Thornmallow wished again he could disappear. It needn't be all the way home. Just outside the room, down the stairs, into the hallway would do. But two days at Wizard's Hall hadn't made him a wizard. Yet.

Magister Hickory pursed his lips and stared up at the balcony. He drew in a great breath. At last he spoke. "Quite . . . right," he said. "You are quite right."

Behind him a sentence burst into a brilliant green, not unlike the color of the lizard soup: YOU MUST TRY.

7

NOT A WIZARD

HEY WERE ALL DISMISSED RIGHT after, and Thornmallow — his knees entirely water — could scarcely keep standing. But with Will and Tansy and Gorse all helping, he finally made his way down the winding stairs.

"Nice going, Thornmallow!" came a call as they reached the main floor. The speaker was an upper-classman with the beginnings of a yellow mustache above his lip.

"Awfully brave, Thorny," cried an older girl, patting him on the head.

"Hurrah, number one-thirteen!" shouted another, waving her hand.

The buzz of student voices was overpowering, and

45

Thornmallow even heard someone say, "Frightfully prickly," which he decided to take as a compliment, though he wasn't entirely sure. But he could feel the heat on his face, and his collar was suddenly too tight, and his knees were still liquid. In truth he was a shy boy and not at all used to crowds.

"I need . . . I need . . . ," he began.

"What you need is air," said Gorse.

He nodded because she was right.

"Make way, make way for the wandy Thornmallow," Will shouted. And surprisingly, an open path appeared between the students. With Will pushing and Tansy pulling and Gorse shouting for everyone to let him be, Thornmallow soon found himself in front of a small wooden door.

"Go on," said Tansy. "Out there. Plenty of air. You need to be alone for a minute. We'll guard the door, and you can get some good breaths."

"Is this — is this what a guardian does?" Thornmallow gasped.

Gorse opened the door. "Of course," she said. "What are you expecting — friends?" But she winked at him before pushing him through and gave him a sunny smile.

Friends, he thought as he walked outside. He'd never actually had any before, just his dear ma and his favorite cow, Bos. *Friends*. If he left now, just disappeared over the Far-Rise Hills, he wouldn't have friends anymore. Except Bos. And his dear ma. All of a sudden, Bos and his dear ma weren't enough.

He breathed deeply seven or eight times, thinking about Will and Tansy and Gorse, before he had the presence of mind to look around. He was back in the very same courtyard he'd entered only the day before. What a barren place it was. No trees. No flowers. No birds singing. And that was odd, for surely wizards could conjure such things. Hadn't he brought in a rosebush on his own? He looked up into the evening sky where the stars had just started to wink on. They stared down at him silently, not at all like the friendly map over his bed, looking as cold and as distant as Magister Hickory.

Magister Hickory! Thornmallow shivered. Magister Hickory had praised him. Well, not exactly praised, but said that what he'd said was *quite right*. Everyone else seemed to think that was praise. But — and Thornmallow smiled ruefully to himself — he hadn't meant to speak out in the meeting any more than he'd meant to bring snow into Magister Beechvale's class.

"Perhaps," he whispered to the barren courtyard, "perhaps I am a brilliant wizard, an enchanter, in spite of myself." He liked the sound of that. It made a certain sense. So he said it a little louder. *"In spite of myself."* After all, he hadn't made up anything, just repeated the verse he'd been taught in class. And repeated the bit of wisdom that first his mother, then

Magister Briar Rose, and Magister Beechvale had said. "Perhaps I *am* wandy. Whatever that is."

Just as a test, he closed his eyes, remembering the little verse about milk and the dry cow. Only, when he opened his mouth and sang it softly to himself, the sound that came out was ghastly:

> There into here,
> Then into now,
> Let down the milk
> From the dry cow.

When he sang it, it wasn't a song. It was too hoarse for that. And it didn't land on any proper note. Or at least any proper *single* note. It wobbled all over the place. As his dear ma often said of him, *Three sounds to the wind and not a one of 'em worth hearing.*

He tried again, a little louder.

If anything, it was worse.

And nothing happened.

"Of course," he whispered to himself, "there's no cow here anyway." But there hadn't been any roses or any snow before he'd sung the other verse in class, and that hadn't stopped the avalanche. At the very least, he'd expected a glass of milk. Or a calf. Or a sight of Bos snug in her barn.

He shook his head. "Not a wizard, then. Except when I *don't* mean it to happen, never mind what rule number five says. There can't be anything *quite right* about that, whatever Magister Hickory thinks. And if I'm here to fill somebody's *desperate need* then that somebody is going to be awfully disappointed."

He would have started crying then, but the door behind him creaked open.

"What's that awful noise?" Gorse called through the crack. "Not blubbing are you? My brothers never blub. My da would whack 'em if they did."

"Are you all right?" That was Tansy.

"Of course he's all right," came Will's voice. "He's better than all right. He's *quite right!*"

The door opened all the way, and there were the three of them, laughing and shaking hands.

Thornmallow walked back inside. "I'm tired," he said. "I'm going to bed." He started down the hallway to the right.

"Not that way!" yelled Gorse. "Unless you want to sleep in the girls' wing."

Thornmallow stopped, his face reddening. Turning, he tried to shrug it off as a joke, but no one was fooled.

"Follow me," Will said, pointing to the left.

He followed Will, but his left and right seemed all mixed up, and he'd lost all sense of direction. He wondered if he'd ever find it again.

"See you in the morning," Tansy called after them. "Third bell. Don't forget."

He tried to make a map of the hallways as they walked, but before he'd gotten anything straight, Will had stopped in front of a small door.

"Your room," Will said.

Thornmallow saw that his name was carved into the door, as well as a picture of a plant he assumed was a thornmallow because it had lines suggesting prickles along the stem. Also the number 113. He sighed.

"Don't take on so," Will said. "We all feel a little bit lost and a little bit lonely first days. That's what the guardians are for. I . . ." He turned and glanced up and down the hallway as if making sure no one was listening. "I even missed my sisters." Then he grinned, a bit sheepishly, and pulled a large blue handkerchief from his pocket. "Here, scrub your nose. You've got a large smudge on it."

"Thanks," Thornmallow said, took the handkerchief, and went into his room, scrubbing his nose.

Everything looked as it had before, except that the picture of his dear ma was different. She was no longer sitting at the butter churn. Instead she was in front of a roaring fire, sewing.

"Oh, Ma, Ma," he whispered, and as if she'd heard him, she looked up for a moment, gazing out past the picture frame. Then she smiled in a satisfied way and looked back down at her work.

For a long time he stared at the picture, hoping it

would move again. When it didn't, he went over to the wardrobe to hang up his jacket. There was a nightshirt on a hook with the initials *TM* on the pocket, and a scholar's robe. Even if *he* wasn't sure he belonged, his room was sure.

"The Bear!" called out the star map overhead.

Thornmallow glanced up at the winking stars. "Hi, Bear," he called back. Then he took off his clothes and hung them carefully on wardrobe pegs, slipped into the nightshirt, and climbed into bed.

"The Crab!" said the map.

"Night, Crab," he mumbled.

Before the ceiling could name a third constellation, Thornmallow was fast asleep.

8

CLASSES

HORNMALLOW WAS AWAKE BE-
fore first bell. By the time the bell
had finished its booming call, he was
out of his nightshirt and into his
clothes. He brushed his teeth and
hair and put on the black scholar's gown. Then he
poked his head out of the door.

The hallway was empty.

Cautiously, he stepped outside his room just as the
second bell rang out, echoing loudly in the corridor.
He could hear the boys starting to stir in their rooms.
Head high, shoulders straight, he walked down the
hallway, checking the names on the doors: *Feverfew
107, Saxifrage 11, Pepperwort 96, Buck's Horne 3.*

The third bell resounded, and doors popped open

all down the corridor. A rush of boys swept past him. One of them was Will.

"Here, Thorny, you're going the wrong way," Will cried, grabbing him by the shoulder and turning him around. "Never go widdershins in anything."

"Widdershins?"

"That's going the opposite direction of the sun's movement, ninny. At Wizard's Hall, only girls can go that way. It's a rule. Number three, actually. Come on." Will shepherded him to the dining room, where the meal was a bowl of thick porridge, clotted cream, and wild strawberries.

"No lizards?" Thornmallow asked.

"Don't even think it. And wipe the side of your nose," said Tansy.

He drew the blue handkerchief out of his pocket and wiped.

The meal was over almost as quickly as it had begun, and Thornmallow was pulled toward a classroom.

"Curses!" whispered Gorse, grinning at him. "It's much better than Elementary Spelling. You'll like it, Thorny. No snow."

They filed in.

Curses *was* much better than Spelling. At least in Curses Thornmallow didn't break down any walls. He learned how to curse a field to blight it, curse a cow to stop its milk, and curse a wart to remove it.

"Much faster than a poultice," Gorse said, "though I heard a third-year named Milkweed got some of the words wrong and managed to lose a toe. It was found in Magister Beechvale's tea."

Tansy gave Gorse such a look that Thornmallow wondered, but it was Will who explained.

"She loves to try and frighten people with her stories," he said.

"Then Milkweed didn't lose a toe?" Thornmallow asked.

"Oh yes," Tansy said. "But not because of the wart." She glared at Gorse.

Gorse grinned. "I was just joking about the tea."

Just then Magister Bledwort called them back to attention, and Thornmallow never did get the rest of the story. And later, when they were changing classes and he tried to ask, they were all much too busy to explain.

Besides, the next class was first-year Names, and he found it much too interesting to remember to ask Gorse about curses, for in this class he learned that all things have a True Name.

"Even me?" he asked timidly, raising his hand.

Magister Hyssop, who taught Names, smiled and nodded her head. "Even you, young Thornwillow."

"Mallow," he corrected automatically.

"No, not Thornmallow. That's not your True

Name at all," Magister Hyssop said. "If it were, you'd have a distinct aura when you spoke it aloud. You are distinctly flat right now. But remember you must take care. Why, class?" She looked around at the hands all waving madly. "Yes, Tansy?"

"True Names," Tansy said, standing as she answered, "must never ever be spoken aloud. That's rule number nine."

"See that you remember that, young Thornapple," cautioned Magister Hyssop. "You never know when the knowledge may be vital."

"Mallow," he said again.

"Not at all," Magister Hyssop replied and turned back to the board.

The idea of finding his True Name so fascinated Thornmallow that he would not let it go. He scarcely listened in the next class, Transformations, even when Will got himself tangled up in a shape-shifting spell and came out with donkey ears, and Wormwood, the blond boy with the hair growing into his ears, turned a strange shade of dark blue. And in Magister Beechvale's Spelling class for the second time, he sat transfixed, whispering a variety of names like a spellmaster out of some ancient tale.

"Dandelion?" he tried. "Fennel? Bachelor's Button? Thyme?" He checked his reflection in the window for an aura, some slight haloing around his head and ears. But he was, in Magister Hyssop's words, *distinctly flat*. And though the list of names he tried went on and on, he saw and felt no change.

At last called upon by Magister Beechvale a second and then a third time, and pinched into awareness by Will from behind, Thornmallow stood.

"Yes, sir," he said, trying to sound as if he knew what was going on.

"I asked, young Thornmolly, if you thought you might try a spell again. Not the snow spell, but another um . . . less active one."

Thornmallow gulped. "Yes, sir," he said in a small voice, setting aside for the moment his search for his True Name. He rose from his seat and went to the front of the class.

This time Magister Beechvale left Thornmallow strictly alone, no hands over the ears, and Thornmallow struggled along. He tried singing and missed each note of the spell by at least a tone and a half. His friends all put their hands over their ears, Wormwood giggled openly, and even Magister Beechvale shook his head.

"Never," the magister muttered. "Never in my fifty years, boy and man, have I heard such sounds. *Never*. What could Dr. Mo have been thinking? And you, our much-needed one hundred and thirteen. We are worse off than before. How could you, young Thornmaple, have brought that snow yesterday? Never. *Never!*"

It was that *never* Thornmallow heard as they marched into the dining hall. It rang louder than any bell. He could not get the sound of it out of his head.

Never. Never. Never.

9

EAVESDROPPING

HORNMALLOW SCARCELY NOTICED what he ate. It could have been real lizard soup for all the attention he paid it. He spent the whole meal wrestling with that voice in his ear.

Never!

It repeated until he was thoroughly sick of it.

Never!

He heard it in Magister Beechvale's strict tones, in Magister Briar Rose's softer ones, and in his own dear ma's familiar voice. It accompanied each slurp of his soup.

Never!

Will tapped him twice on the shoulder. "Thorny — what's wrong?"

Thornmallow looked up as if in a daze. "What?"

"You're muttering to yourself," said Tansy.

"And saying nothing worth repeating," Gorse added.

The other first-years at the table giggled, and Wormwood pulled at the yellow hairs invading his right ear.

"Never!" Thornmallow said. "They're right."

"Who are *they?*" Tansy whispered to Gorse, who shrugged.

"I'll *never* make a wizard. Never in four years; never in a million and four years. I'm going to Magister Hickory right now to tell him it's best for everyone if I quit."

"*Not* a wizard?" asked Tansy. "But what about that avalanche of snow?"

"And the roses on top?" added Will.

"What about *quite right* and trying?" asked Gorse. "And the fact that you are number one-thirteen? All the magisters seem to think that's terribly important."

Up and down the table, all the first-years were listening in to the conversation and nodding. Even Wormwood.

"It's all a terrible mistake," explained Thornmallow, standing. He could feel the soup — whatever kind it was — swimming around inside his stomach. *Probably doing the backstroke*, a little voice in his head said, and at that the soup lurched and threatened to come back up. "A mistake," he said loud enough so that everyone up and down the table could hear. "And the snow and roses were Magister Beechvale's doing, not mine."

Before anyone could tell him no, he stepped over the bench and walked out of the dining hall.

Turning left — never widdershins as Will had warned — he walked down the corridor and soon found himself in front of a series of doors neatly labeled with the names of the magisters. He let out a long breath, and that was the first time he knew he'd been holding it.

"Magister Beechvale, Register Oakbend, Magister Lilybell, Magister Briar Rose . . . ," he whispered aloud as he passed each door. He hesitated at Briar Rose's, remembering how nice she'd been and wondering for just a moment if he should ask for her advice. Then, shaking his head, he walked on.

At last he came to a door with MAGISTER HICK-ORY in gold. He raised his fist and was about to knock, when he heard voices coming from inside the room.

Now, Thornmallow was not an eavesdropping sort of boy. At home there had been no one but cows and chickens to eavesdrop on. So it wasn't in his nature, and he hadn't acquired it as a habit. There was never any thought, therefore, that he should listen. On the other hand, there wasn't any thought that he shouldn't, especially since the very first words he could make out included his name.

"That Thornfellow is the last," came a voice.

"Mallow," corrected another. (He thought it might be Magister Briar Rose.)

"Prickly on the outside, squishy within, but he does try hard." (Probably Magister Beechvale.)

"*Squark!*"

"So now we have the necessary number." (Clearly that was Magister Hickory, with a voice of authority.)

"*And* thirteen magisters." (Magister Hyssop.)

"Just in time," pronounced Magister Hickory, "as Dr. Mo promised. Though I do think that was cutting it a bit fine."

Cutting? Fine? Thornmallow wondered what Magister Hickory meant.

As if in answer to the unspoken question, Magister Hickory continued, "The Quilted Beast and its Master will come on the night of the next full moon, which is . . ." He hesitated as if calculating. "Tomorrow. So it is written. So it must be. Register Oakbend checked and rechecked our calculations, using the letters in the Beast's name. One hundred and thirteen was the number needed, and so he sent out the Call. Thornmellow answered it."

"Mallow," said Magister Briar Rose.

"But what do we do with that number?" Magister

Hyssop's lilting voice asked. "The spell is unclear. And what good are we anyway, already so diminished by the Master and his beast?"

"*Squark!*"

"Dr. Mo is right, Hyssop. We must try." Magister Hickory's voice sounded a positive note. "As to what we do with that number — if we knew the answer to that, my dear, we would not be in such danger. All we know is that we had to reach precisely one hundred and thirteen students, and Thornwillow is it. With the boy here, the Beast's defeat is at least *possible*. And the Master's. Without Thornbellow, Wizard's Hall is — " Magister Hickory's voice suddenly stopped. "What was that?"

Behind the closed door, Thornmallow had moaned out loud. He hadn't meant to, but the sound had escaped his mouth without his willing it.

The door was flung open.

"Thornpillow!" said Magister Hickory.

"Marrow," corrected Magister Beechvale.

"Mallow," squeaked Thornmallow.

"You were *eavesdropping!*" Magister Hickory's face was as red as an apple.

"I — I didn't mean to, sir. It's just . . . it's just . . ." Thornmallow stood transfixed, his mouth refusing to say the rest of the words. He felt terrifically squishy inside.

"*Squark!*"

Magister Hickory took a step back, and his mouth assumed a more welcoming expression. "Better come in, boy."

At that, all Thornmallow had been feeling and worrying about rushed up to his tongue. He couldn't have followed Magister Hickory's invitation to move if he'd been threatened with a hot poker, but he *could* speak.

"Please, sir. I was just here to tell you that I realize I will never make a wizard, no matter *how* hard I try. I can't find the dominant, and I'm not very practical, and hardly ever punctual. And I thought it best, really sir, for everyone if I left. Now. Today. At once. Except . . ."

There was an awful hush in the room.

"Except?" Magister Hickory's voice was suddenly like thunder over the Far-Rise Hills.

"Except," Thornmallow added miserably, his voice breaking on the two syllables, "I *did* hear what you said. Without meaning to, that is."

The magisters looked at one another in great concern. Thornmallow continued uneasily.

"If I leave, you will no longer have the one hundred and thirteen students you need. And somehow you need that number because of some beast and its master. And you need that number by tomorrow night.

And we can't count on another Call, I suppose, going out in time, and some other boy or girl showing up." His voice got somewhat wistful here and he looked at the magisters, all of whom were shaking their heads.

"So though I am certainly no kind of hero, being small and thin and often smudgy of nose . . ." He rubbed his fist over his nose. "I could stay until just after you defeat this beast fellow. And its master. You know I *was* able to make some snow yesterday, and maybe that might help. If you need snow, that is. Though I know I need more practice. And then . . ." His voice trailed off, though by a supreme act of will, he managed to keep it from whimpering.

"Squark!"

Register Oakbend turned his sightless eyes toward Thornmallow, and those eyes pierced right through him. He could feel the sharp pinpricks where they entered.

"Dr. Mo says you *must* stay." Register Oakbend closed his eyes, and Thornmallow felt as if the pins had been removed.

"Till . . . till when?"

Before anyone could answer, the room suddenly went dark. Not the kind of dark that happens if the light has been turned off, but as dark as if *all* light and *all* color were gone from the world for good. And there was an odd smell, of something wet and old and horrible.

Just as suddenly, the smell was gone, and the light came back on.

"What was that?" whispered Thornmallow.

"The Master has been playing with us for a full week now," said Magister Hickory softly. "Lights on and off, odd noises, awful smells. And that was a glimpse of the Beast."

Remembering the lights going off in Magister Briar Rose's room, Thornmallow said, "But I saw nothing."

"Which is worse — seeing or not seeing?" asked Register Oakbend.

Shivering, Thornmallow said, "But the smell . . ." He gulped. "It was like a bear's winter cave. Like a sick cow's breath. Like . . ."

"Better not remark any more upon it," cautioned Magister Briar Rose. "In Wizard's Hall, things spoken aloud can become real."

"And names have power," added Magister Hyssop.

Thornmallow nodded grimly. "I'll stay," he said. He wondered if they could see the trembling of his knees beneath his gown, then decided that, since they were wizards, they probably could. "I'll stay. And I'll try."

"Good boy," called out Register Oakbend. "Dr. Mo knew you'd do."

Magister Hickory walked over to Thornmallow and

put an arm around his shoulder. "Now, child, none of this must get beyond this door. We haven't told the other students because we don't want to cause a panic. Do you understand? Can't have even one of the one hundred and thirteen leaving Wizard's Hall in fright. Clearly we need all of you. It's in the rules of the spell."

"What rules?" Thornmallow asked. "What spell?" It was an incredibly brave thing to do, asking that question with Magister Hickory's arm on his shoulder. He was to wonder ever after how he managed it.

"All magic — even dark magic like the Master's — has to follow rules and *be fair*. The spell the Master gave us goes this way." He closed his eyes and sang — on the dominant, Thornmallow was sure:

> Ever on the quilting goes,
> Spinning out the lives between,
> Winding up the souls of those
> Students up to one-thirteen.

"That's all we know, and it should be enough. But you can understand why we have to guard against even one student leaving now," said Magister Hickory. "One hundred and thirteen students. That's what the spell says we have to have. Don't you see?"

He didn't, really. But because Magister Hickory's arm was around him, and because he had been spoken to as if he were truly one of them, he found that after a while he did see. Truly.

10

TELLING TALES

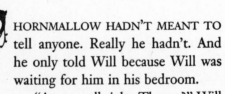HORNMALLOW HADN'T MEANT TO tell anyone. Really he hadn't. And he only told Will because Will was waiting for him in his bedroom.

"Are you all right, Thorny?" Will asked, sitting with his legs tucked under him on the bed. "You look like my sister Mairsie does whenever she fibs. Or my sister Maisie does when she has fallen out of love." He looked carefully at Thornmallow. "And that happens to them both all the time."

Thornmallow nodded unhappily.

"The Seven Sis —" the star map began, stopping abruptly when Will shot his right pinky up in the air.

"How did you do that?" Thornmallow asked. "And why? I like the map and the way it says the star names."

"I did it so we can talk, Thorny," Will said. "Without interruption from on high, so to speak." When he saw Thornmallow's face, he added, "That's a joke." Then he held up his left hand. "If you want to start it again, you jab your left pinky up like this." The map began again.

" — ters," it said. "The Bear."

Thornmallow put his right pinky in the air. Nothing happened. The map kept speaking, running through two names and starting on a third. "The Big Dip —"

"Here!" said Will, grabbing Thornmallow's hand and jabbing it upward. "Give it a little *oomph!*"

The map stopped in midname with a peculiar popping, almost like a hiccup.

"Now, what's this all *really* about, Thorny?" Will asked, shaking his head and looking so sympathetic that Thornmallow spilled out the whole story before he could stop himself.

"*Whush!*" Will said, lying back on the bed and staring up at the star map. He wrinkled his nose as if he himself were smelling the Beast. Above him the lights of the silent map glowed steadily. "And they really said that tomorrow was the day?"

"Tomorrow night, actually." Thornmallow sat down heavily at the foot of the bed, and his hands wrangled together.

For a long moment Will was silent. Needing the reassurance of words, Thornmallow stuck his left pinky in the air with as much *oomph* as he could muster. But the map, too, was silent.

At last Will sat up. "Only the magisters and you know about this?"

Thornmallow nodded glumly. "They didn't want a panic," he said. "So only the magisters and I — and you — know. I sort of promised not to tell," he added miserably.

"Then I sort of promise not to tell anyone else," Will said. "Or panic." He swung his legs over the side of the bed and stood. "The Quilted Beast. And his Master. *Whush*. I'll have to think about that! Good night." He rose.

"Will . . . ," Thornmallow began.

"What?"

"Could you start the stars again? I like to go to sleep while they're still talking."

"Just put your hand up," Will said. "Your left hand. Left pinky."

Thornmallow did. When nothing happened, Will grabbed his hand and jerked it upward.

" — per!" said the stars, rather more loudly than before.

"Easy, see?" said Will. "Any first-year can do it. Oh, and can I have my handkerchief back now? Your nose is clean."

Thornmallow pulled it from his pocket, crumpled and smudgy, and Will smoothed it out, shook it, and the smudges fell off on the floor. Then he slid the handkerchief back into his pocket, and left the room.

The next morning Thornmallow got up at the bell. His scholar's robe was freshly pressed and hanging in the closet. He put on his clothes and, with the hem of the robe flapping about his ankles, was in the hallway by second bell.

"Today's the day," shouted Tansy at the first turning.

"Tonight's the night," added Gorse mysteriously.

"For what?" A cold chill started down Thornmallow's spine.

"*You* know," they answered together, their voices purposefully eerie.

When he caught up with Will, Thornmallow grabbed him by the sleeve. "You promised!" he whispered furiously.

"Promised what?"

"Not to tell."

"Tell what?"

"About the Beast. And its Master."

"I only told Tansy," Will said.

"And I only told Gorse," Tansy added, catching up to them.

"And I never promised anything," said Gorse, panting a little as she came up behind. "Though I just heard, so I haven't had time to tell anyone else."

"Well, you mustn't. This isn't a game. It isn't fun . or funny. It is serious and dangerous." Thornmallow was shaking with a combination of anger and dread.

"Listen, Thornmallow," Gorse began, "*all* magic is serious and dangerous. Which is not to say you can't have fun with it as well."

"You didn't smell the Beast. You didn't hear the magisters. I did. But I wasn't supposed to tell, and now I have got to find Magister Hickory and confess that I did."

"Bad idea," warned Gorse. "Confess to a wizard, and you'll get swat for sure. Trust me. My da is a — "

"Bush wizard. Yes, we know all about him, Gorse," said Will. "But we've all let Thorny down. Especially me. Going with him to see Magister Hickory is the least we can do. And if it means a punishment, then we've got it coming."

He dragged Thornmallow off to the left, and Tansy dragged Gorse to the right. They met around the next corner and walked four-abreast down the hall. At the corridor's end was a big door with Magister Hickory's name carved in gold on the crosspiece, jets of lightning streaking down each side.

"That's a different door from yesterday," Thornmallow said suspiciously.

"Of course," said Gorse. "This is a different day."

"You can't expect it to stay the same," Tansy added. "Not at Wizard's Hall."

It was then they heard the voice, dark and infinitely cold, behind the door.

"That's . . . ," Thornmallow began. Then the iciness of the voice sealed his lips, and he couldn't say anything more.

11

THE MASTER SPEAKS

ROM UNDER THE BIG DOOR AND around its edges, a dark cold voice seeped out, enveloping them. At first the words were lost in the dark and the cold. But after a moment they could make out what was being said.

"TONIGHT!" the voice said.

Next to that awful voice, Magister Hickory's answer was tiny, tinny, and weak. "We have the number to defeat you. We have the requisite one hundred and thirteen."

The voice laughed.

"It sounds like cobwebs in corners," whispered Will.

"It sounds like shouts down a rain barrel," whispered Tansy.

"It sounds like distant thunder up close," whispered Gorse.

Thornmallow was silent. What it sounded like to him was *doom*, but he didn't say that. He was remembering what Magister Briar Rose had told him — that things said aloud in Wizard's Hall could become real. He had already broken one promise to Magister Hickory — the one about telling. He would not break the other. He *would* try.

Working hard at smiling, Thornmallow winked at his friends. It was the longest, the most difficult wink he ever managed. "Cows," he said. "Cows sound like that—MOOOOOO. MOOOOOO. And we milk them." He wondered if saying *that* aloud would have any effect.

Gorse snapped, "You don't understand, Thornmallow. This is *serious*. Whoever that is has The Voice. Only the greatest of Magisters has The Voice."

"And I say that voice sounds like cows," Thornmallow said again.

"Bet you know a lot about cows," said Gorse.

"I know more about cows than magic," Thornmallow answered.

Tansy put a hand on both their shoulders. "Why are you two arguing?" she asked.

"MOOOOOO!" Thornmallow said, determined to get the last word in. All of a sudden they all laughed. Somehow his clowning had relaxed them.

But no sooner had they sighed their little bit of relief than the cold, dark voice began again.

"One hundred and thirteen, Hickorystick? Mere numbers do not impress me. But I will *im*-press you. We will meet again in the Great Hall at midnight, and then you will see how little I care for your puny magicks and your useless spells. You thought once I was not good enough to run your miserable Hall. But now I will run my Beast through it and enjoy the sight."

This time the laugh that accompanied The Voice shook splinters from the door, and the gold lightning jets fell out, clattering at their feet. A clap of thunder shook the walls. Will and Gorse fell to the ground, hands over their ears. Tansy grabbed Thornmallow's fingers and squeezed them until he felt sure the bones cried out.

Then the door flew open. The four of them melted back against the wall, trying to act like paint.

Out stumbled Magister Hickory, his great mane of hair lying limp on his shoulders. His handsome face seemed like ancient parchment stretched over gaunt bones. Stooping, he felt for the wall with one palsied hand.

"Magister Hickory!" cried Thornmallow, rushing to him. "What can we do to help?"

"What can *you* do?" Magister Hickory looked old and confused. There was a tremor building in his lower lip.

"We can run," said Gorse, quite definitely.

"We can hide," said Will.

"We can do what Thornmallow said," Tansy whispered.

Magister Hickory turned toward her uncertainly, his lusterless eyes afraid. "What is that, child?"

"We can try," Tansy whispered.

Thornmallow reached for her hand. It felt warm and safe in his. "Yes," he said, "we can try." Saying it aloud like that made it real.

They surrounded Magister Hickory, touching his hands and arms. "Yes, we can," they cried out together. "We can try."

Slowly Magister Hickory straightened up. He ran a hand tentatively through his mane of hair. His eyes began to clear, and he looked at his students one at a time, as if drawing strength from their eager faces. At last he said, "Did you hear The Voice?"

Thornmallow spoke for them all. "We heard, sir."

"And what it said?"

Gorse added, "We did."

"And still you will try?"

Together they said, "We will."

Magister Hickory touched each of their faces in turn, as if assuring himself they were really there, not some bit of magic forced upon him by his enemy. The last face he touched was Thornmallow's. He smiled, which made his lower lip stop trembling.

"Then so will I, my children," he said, his voice getting stronger with each word. "So will I."

12

THE STORY OF THE BEAST

GUESS I'D BETTER TELL YOU THE story of the Master and the Beast, then," Magister Hickory said. "Come into my room and sit down. The story is long and not at all pleasant."

"Will . . . he . . . be back?" Tansy asked.

"The Master? No, not until tonight. He did what he came to do — to trade threats with me," said Magister Hickory. "As you well know, so much of magic is in the head. And this visit has drained him."

"He didn't sound drained to me," said Gorse.

Magister Hickory managed another, smaller smile. It didn't reassure any of them. "Remember your first lessons in appearances, child."

The others nodded uneasily, but Thornmallow did

79

not. Magister Hickory's hair was still hanging limp on his shoulders and his fingers kept trembling at his sides. For all the wizard's talk, *he* was the one who looked drained. As a farm boy, Thornmallow knew to check such things as hair and limbs. Didn't his dear ma always say, *A cow's tail tells you more than her mouth*. If that was the *appearance* of what the Master could do . . .

The magister's room was not what Thornmallow was expecting. It was not the office of the evening before but a bedroom, warm and homey. There was a small slant-top desk against a window overlooking a rolling hillside. A pair of red plush slippers sat heel-to-toe under the four-poster bed. Magister Hickory had obviously been reading in bed, for there were three open books lying on the quilt. Thornmallow could see that one was a book of spells, one a book of numbers, and one was about herbalry, for the picture on the page was of a bunch of dill plants crowned with lavender flowers.

On the wall next to the bed were a dozen portraits. Thornmallow recognized a few of them as magisters. One picture especially drew his eye. It was of the most beautiful woman he had ever seen, her dark hair cascading down either side of a heart-shaped face, framing it. He turned to ask about the picture and saw that the others were already sitting down, Gorse on a footstool, Tansy on a hassock, and Will on the floor. Magister Hickory had settled into a large overstuffed chair. Hastily Thornmallow folded himself cross-legged next to Will.

"The story starts, my children, back before you were born. Back at the beginning of Wizard's Hall," Magister Hickory said. The words rolled out of his mouth like a chant. As he spoke, the life seemed to return to his eyes, and his hair began to lift ever so slowly, strand by strand, from his shoulders.

Thornmallow remembered what Register Oakbend had said. *Words mean something.* And clearly, as Magister Hickory spoke, the very act of speaking the words, telling the story, re-creating another time, gave him life. Just as the words spoken by the awful Master had brought him a kind of death.

"Wizard's Hall was begun by fourteen of us, magic-makers from all over the Dales. I had just graduated in spell-making from the Castle of the Divine. Magister Briar Rose had been a simple herbwife of some fame in Shepardston. Register Oakbend had been a necromancer of no small knowledge in Seddingham-over-the-Hill. And then there was Magister Morning Glory." He turned his head toward the pictures on the wall, and the portrait of the beautiful woman seemed to smile ever so slightly.

"Morning Glory was a Doctor of Divining," Magister Hickory said, his voice soft with remembering. "And she was the most accomplished of us all. In

fact it was she who had the idea for Wizard's Hall
and she who sent out the original Call, a Call so strong
and so pure that we thirteen — a wizard's dozen — who
answered it all agreed it could not be denied." He sat
up straight in the chair, then leaned forward toward
them.

Thornmallow glanced over at the portrait of Magister Morning Glory. The smile was gone.

"What was begun in harmony ended in tragedy,"
Magister Hickory said and then slowly sank back
against the chair.

"What happened?" asked Will into the silence.

"What indeed." Magister Hickory's voice was now
so quiet, the four children had to lean toward him to
hear. He took an enormous pocket handkerchief from
the air, flourished it once, and blew his nose loudly, a
sound unaccountably like a trumpet. At a second blow,
the handkerchief disappeared. "What indeed."

"What indeed . . . ," prompted Gorse.

Magister Hickory drew in a deep breath and sat
up straight once again. This time his hair stood out
around his head like a lion's mane, and his eyes were
fierce.

"One of our original members was a wizard named
Nettle from Overton-Across-the-Waters. Though he
was an accomplished magician, he was well named.
He was prickly, both outside and in. At first he was
quiet, well-mannered even. But soon enough, we

learned his real character. His words stung, and he loved to use them in anger. Still, we were thirteen, and he was one. But when we voted him out of the Hall, he began to study the black arts long into the night. In his nightwork he conjured up a Beast from the black side of our souls. Bit by bit, he quilted that Beast together, until it had swallowed up — "

"Excuse me," said Thornmallow, his voice soft with fear, "but I don't understand."

Magister Hickory nodded. "Of course you don't, young Thornswallow. You have only been here a few days."

"I mean — wouldn't it be a good idea to lose the black side? That way, your souls could shine all pure as gold? And it's Thorn*mallow*. Sir."

Magister Hickory smiled indulgently. "By 'black,' my prickly friend, I do not mean evil. Or wicked. I mean dark and deep, as in the black water of the deepest lakes. All those *strongest of emotions* that — if used improperly — tempt us to wicked, evil deeds. For example, ambition, which can become greed. Or desire, which can become gluttony. Or admiration, which can become envy. We are all made up of such deep and dark emotions, and as we grow more mature, we learn to control them."

Thornmallow nodded, remembering how often his dear ma said, *Good folk think bad thoughts; bad folk act on 'em.*

83

Magister Hickory nodded back. "Even love can have a black side. Even love."

"So what happened?" Gorse asked.

"Those of us with smaller black sides, smaller emotions, we lost little and could still function, if somewhat less sharply than before," said Magister Hickory. "Why, once you could hear me from one side of the Hall to the other. And Magister Briar Rose — her laughter could lift a tree. But now . . ." He shook his head. "Still, we had little to lose compared to our dear Morning Glory. And she — well, she disappeared."

They all spoke together.

Will said, "You mean . . ."

Gorse said, "Then where's . . ."

Tansy said, "Is that why . . ."

But it was Thornmallow's question that rang out above the rest. "So has she gone entirely?"

"Gone — and not gone," Magister Hickory said. He rose suddenly and walked over to the wall, where he plucked down the picture of the beautiful woman and stared at it. "Gone — and not gone."

"But she couldn't have had a worse black side than the rest of you," cried Thornmallow, who was already half in love with the picture.

"She had more ambition, more insight, more desire than all of us," said Magister Hickory, shaking his head. "And more love." He placed the picture facedown on the little table by the chair. "And tonight when the Master — who was once the wizard Magister Nettle — comes with the Quilted Beast by his side, he will loose his powerful spells. And he will slowly leach out the rest of our strong emotions, feeding them to his Quilted Beast, making it grow huge with our stolen feelings. If we cannot stop him, we who are the best and the brightest in the land, he will make us all disappear, and he will then own Wizard's Hall. From there, why, he could go on to own all of the Dales."

Thornmallow leaped to his feet, filled with unaccountable bravery. He was thinking of his new friends here in the room. He was thinking of the magisters and Register Oakbend and the little white creature in the cage. He was thinking about his dear ma, no longer safe in her cozy home. What he was not thinking about was what he was going to say. It just popped out on its own.

"Tell us what to do!" he cried. "We will not fail you."

Magister Hickory's head, like a clockwork figure's, began to shake back and forth, back and forth. "Oh, my dear children," he said in time to each shake. "It may be we who will fail you — for, though we know we need one hundred and thirteen students to break the Master's hold, we do not know *what* to do."

13

IDEAS

OR A LONG MOMENT NO ONE spoke. Thornmallow could feel a kind of heat rising to his cheeks, and behind his eyes unshed tears prickled.

At last Magister Hickory stood, his voice soft as a cradle song. "Without a good breakfast," he said, "we will none of us have the strength for tonight's work."

"Whatever *that* shall be," murmured Thornmallow, but he was all of a sudden hungry, as if the magister's suggestion had been spoken directly to his stomach.

The four children rose and filed out of the room, boys turning left, girls right, but Magister Hickory did not follow. Instead he closed the door softly behind them.

Thornmallow was not surprised to find himself suddenly in front of the dining hall, side by side with the other three. They glanced briefly at one another before going in. None of them remarked on Magister Hickory's absence.

"I hope," Thornmallow said, trying to change the mood, "I hope it isn't lizard soup."

In fact it was porridge, a lighter shade of brown than the soup, and when Tansy mentioned raisins, they immediately popped up like freckles in the bowls. Thornmallow wished she had mentioned strawberries instead. But when he tasted his porridge he realized it was just the appearance and not the actual fruit, so it didn't matter after all.

The four of them stumbled through Elementary Spelling and Curses and first-year Names, their attention wandering. They kept giving one another little frightened, rabbity looks. However, their distraction was hardly noticed. The magisters, too, seemed unable to concentrate on the lessons, and the classes became strange combinations of badly articulated questions and barely understood answers.

None of the magicks worked.

It was rather like a half-holiday, only they were still in their seats.

———

At lunch the strange mood at Wizard's Hall was all anyone talked about. One of the fourth-year students remarked, "I've never seen anything like it."

When they went back to Transformation class, there was a note on the door:

CANCELED ON ACCOUNT

"On account of what?" asked Wormwood, fiddling with his ear.

No one had an answer.

"That's done it!" Will whispered to Thornmallow. "Now everyone will want to know why."

Thornmallow turned to Will. "They *should* be told," he whispered back. "To be fair."

"To be fair," Gorse said, her voice too loud by half, "we should all be sent home."

"Sent home?" Wormwood insinuated himself into their circle. "But why?"

"Because . . . ," Gorse began, but she was elbowed fiercely by Will.

"Because," Tansy finished for her, "if we're to have an undeclared holiday, it would be more fun at home."

Satisfied, Wormwood left to spread the rumor that they were all going to get the afternoon off. It took the magisters the rest of the day to make sure none of the one hundred and thirteen students actually left.

Magister Briar Rose had to run after two second-year students who'd made it as far as the gates with a picnic basket chock-full of egg-and-watercress sandwiches.

"Of course," Tansy said, "I really have no home to go to. Except for Wizard's Hall."

"Her ma and da are dead," Gorse explained to Thornmallow. "And mine are away on a business trip. Wizards' business."

"Mine still have farmwork to do," Will said. "They *could* use a helping hand."

Thornmallow thought about his own dear ma and about running off home to her. He knew she'd velcome him. But running off home wouldn't be right. After all, he *had* promised. And he *had* to try.

Suddenly Thornmallow looked up. "What are we talking about? There *is* no holiday. It was just something Tansy said to get rid of Wormwood."

As if coming up out of a dream, the three stared at him.

"You're right," Will said. "What *have* we been talking about?"

"It's a magic drain," Gorse whispered fiercely. "My da told me about them. Pulls all sense out of you and leaves only non-sense. It must be the result of the Master's stopping by."

"Well, what can we do?" Thornmallow asked. "To help the magisters, I mean. To defeat the Master and the Beast?"

"We're only first-years," reminded Tansy, putting her hand on Thornmallow's shoulder.

"But we must try," he exclaimed.

Tansy's eyes widened suddenly. "Try? Of course we'll try!"

"How?" asked Will.

Thornmallow grabbed up his hand. "Think, Will, think!"

Will's mouth opened and shut twice, like a fish in a shallow pool. "The library," he gasped out at last.

"To learn things," agreed Tansy, tightening her grip on Thornmallow's shoulder.

"You're all crazy," Gorse said, turning to leave. But Will caught her by the arm and pulled her around. She stared at him. "What things?"

"Things like . . . nettles," Tansy said.

"And correspondences," added Will.

Understanding seemed suddenly to dawn on Gorse. "I'll take nettles or quilts."

It's as if they are all speaking another language, Thornmallow thought miserably. *And only I'm left out.* He made a wry face, remembering something his dear ma always said, *Secrets is like wounds, can't be cleansed until opened.*

"Let's go!" cried Will, and dragging Thornmallow to the left, he turned the corner, and they were there.

14

LIBRARY TIME

'LL TAKE NETTLES," GORSE SAID.

"I'll take quilts," said Tansy.

"I'll look up correspondences," said Will, shutting the library door carefully behind them.

Thornmallow looked around. The library had walls of books. There were books on the windowsills and books stacked two- and three- and four-deep on shelves. Where there were no books, single pieces of parchment littered the floor, covered with crabbed writings and odd diagrams with arrows pointing up and down and around great circles.

Nettles. And quilts. And correspondences. What did they mean? And where did they mean to start? Thornmallow couldn't move. He stood, amazed.

91

As if she knew exactly where to go and what to do, Gorse headed for a particular wall of books and began pulling down volumes, two at a time. Tansy gathered up books from a great plum-covered chair near an oriel window. Will shuffled through leaves of parchment as if they were cards in a deck.

"What *are* you all doing?" Thornmallow asked at last, no longer caring if they knew how stupid he felt.

"Finding out, of course," Gorse said in an exasperated tone.

"Finding out *what?*"

For a moment they all looked so puzzled at his puzzlement that Thornmallow drew in a deep breath. At last he let it out and said, "Look — I know I'm new here. Why, I didn't even know there *was* a library. So how can I help it if I don't know why we are looking up nettles and quilts and . . . and . . . correspondences?"

Gorse shook her head as if appalled at his ignorance, but Tansy dropped the books back onto the plum-colored chair. Dust flew up and then settled gently back down on the cushion.

Crossing the room, Tansy explained in a singsong voice, chanting a verse as if she were in class:

> Correspondence is the key
> To making dreams reality.

First you must repeat the name;
Then make the magic be the same.

"Get it?" she asked in a normal voice.

Dismally, Thornmallow shook his head.

"Thorn . . . mallow," Tansy said in a quiet but determined way. "Now do you get it?"

"No."

"Why do you suppose that's your name, stupid?" Gorse called.

He turned and glared at her. "Because I'm supposed to be prickly on the outside," he answered sharply. "Or so everyone keeps telling me." His chin began to quiver and his eyes shone with tears.

Tansy smiled. "And squishy within. Just like a thornmallow. You are like your name, and it is like you. They *correspond*."

"Like Tansy is named Tansy because she has such a sunny disposition," said Gorse. "And Willoweed because he manages to plant himself anywhere. Just like willoweed."

"And Gorse is . . . ," Tansy began.

"Small and prickery," Gorse finished, as if proud of it.

"So," Will said, "if we understand what a nettle is, all its properties and uses, then we will understand all about the *wizard* Nettle — what he is." His busy fingers kept at the parchments. "And we'll be able to take away his nettlesome nature."

"Make *him* squishy within?" asked Thornmallow.

All three spoke at once: "Exactly."

"And if we learn all about making quilts," Gorse added, never looking away from the bookcase, "we'll also learn how to *un*-quilt the Beast."

"It all sounds too easy," Thornmallow said. "And The Voice we heard is not going to be overcome with easy magic. Besides, if *we* thought of it, why didn't the magisters?"

"Probably because it *is* too simple and too easy," Gorse said. "Have you ever noticed how grown-ups try to complicate everything? Make it harder than it is? Like grown-up food, with too many sauces."

"And grown-up clothes, with too many buttons," added Tansy.

"And grown-up manners," Will said. "With too many *shoulds* and *shouldn'ts*."

Thornmallow nodded. It all made sense in a way. But something still was troubling him. "WAIT!"

They all looked at him.

"Thornmallow isn't my True Name. Nor is Henry. No auras, remember? Distinctly flat. I mean — Nettle can't be the wizard's True Name. He'd never let anyone know it. So if we don't know his True Name, what good are all these correspondences anyway?"

Will dropped the parchments to the floor and sank

down next to them. Gorse turned from the bookcase, looking grim. Tansy's hands flapped like broken wings.

"He's right, you know," Tansy said at last. "Why didn't *we* think of that?"

They shook their heads slowly.

Tansy added, "Without knowing Nettle's True Name, we might as well not even try."

The library seemed to reflect their depression. The light appeared to dim, and the walls became as somber as the leather bindings of the books. The words *not even try* hung in the air, heavy as the smell of the Beast.

"NOT EVEN TRY?" For the first time since coming to Wizard's Hall, Thornmallow raised his voice. "NOT EVEN TRY?" He remembered his mother's face at the window.

"Magister Hickory didn't mention Nettle knowing the True Names of the magisters. So if Nettle managed all he did without knowing them, why can't we?"

No one answered.

"Gorse, you take nettles as planned. And Tansy, quilts," Thornmallow said. There was a new power in his voice.

The library lights shot back up to full strength, and the walls brightened again to an off-white.

"Right — and I'll continue with correspondences," Will agreed. "I've already located a bit about it on

95

one of these parchments." He scrabbled through the crackling amber-colored sheets. "Here!" He pulled one out of the pile, smiling triumphantly.

"And what about you, Thornmallow?" asked Gorse, clutching a brown book to her chest. "What will you do?"

"I don't really know yet," Thornmallow admitted.

"Well, at least you can *try* to help me," Gorse said. She winked and held out the book. "Chapter two seems to have lots about nettles in it. See what you can make of it."

15

FULL MOON NIGHT

HORNMALLOW READ FOR HOURS, first to himself and then, when he found he was skipping paragraphs, aloud. "The Common or Great Nettle and the Small Nettle grow profusely upon waste ground and along otherwise barren waysides." He looked up at Tansy, who was sitting cross-legged on the plum-colored chair, deep in her seventeenth book. "Do you suppose he's a Small or a Great Nettle? He's certainly not Common."

"Read it to yourself," Gorse snapped from the window ledge. "The rest of us are trying to concentrate."

"Sorry." Thornmallow looked down again at the book and read the next twenty pages to himself, his lips moving, as if that might help him memorize the information. He was careful not to read aloud again. "Nettles are covered with stinging hairs." He tried to imagine a wizard covered with stinging hairs. The very thought made him shiver.

Turning to the center of the book, he looked at several colored pictures of nettles: the creeping roots, the leaves on opposite sides of the stems, the flowers small and green. He discovered that Great Nettle was also called Blind Nettle, Deaf Nettle, False Nettle, Dead Nettle, Red Nettle, White Nettle, Bee Nettle, and Hedge. It was a prolixity of names. He wondered, briefly, if any of them were important.

"Nettles," he read further, "may be boiled and eaten as a remedy against scurvy. The leaves and roots, cut small or granulated, in a cup of boiling water make a tincture that, when taken cold, one cup a day, is a valuable decoction against sick stomachs." Quietly he sounded out the words he didn't know. He understood little of it.

Finally, putting the book facedown on a large library table, Thornmallow went over to Will, who crouched on the floor, his finger tapping a passage on one of the many parchment leaves spread about him.

"Will," Thornmallow whispered, "there's lots and lots about nettles. But nothing seems to make sense if I try to apply it to our wizard Nettle. Except, perhaps, that they all have stinging hairs and a nasty reputa-

tion. The chief thing a nettle seems to do is to irritate
or annoy or vex a person."

"*You* are irritating and annoying and vexing me,"
said Will, not even looking up from the parchment.
"And *you* are not a nettle. Leave me alone, Thorny.
I'm reading up on correspondences, and this is my
thirtieth parchment. I've almost got it, I think. But
it's real difficult. Fourth-year stuff."

But whatever it was that Will had almost got now
evidently got away again, for not a moment later he
stood and stretched, shaking his head. Tansy stood
too, kicking her legs about as if waking them up from
a very long nap.

"Look!" Gorse cried out suddenly from the window ledge. She pointed outside.

A full moon — red and round as a copper coin —
was just beginning to rise.

"But it can't be that late," Tansy complained.

Thornmallow swung around and stared at the library clock. Its hands circled its face frantically, as if
all time had suddenly been compressed.

"That's not right," he said. "And not fair. I thought
magic — even dark magic — had to be fair."

"A fair chance," Will explained. "Not fair."

"And look!" Gorse cried again, pressing her nose
against the glass. "Everything outside is now a barren
waste."

"Where nettles grow . . . ," Thornmallow mumbled, moving to the window for a closer look. "But," he added, remembering how bare the grounds had looked when he first arrived, "wasn't it *always* this way?"

"Oh no!" they all said.

Tansy added, "Wizard's Hall is known far and wide for its flowers and gardens and trees."

"Magic makes things grow wonderfully," Will said.

"Better than compost," put in Gorse.

Shaking his head, Thornmallow looked thoughtful. "That's very odd," he said. "There were no gardens or flowers or trees when *I* arrived." It was as if the Hall were already being prepared for nettles. *If that is dark magic*, he told himself, *then I don't like it at all.*

Then Thornmallow remembered something Tansy had said when they had talked about the lizard soup. Something about *balance*. Big with little, up with down, soft with loud. *Fast with slow.* She hadn't mentioned that one particularly, but it made sense. "Fast with slow," he said aloud. "Balance. Think how slowly time went for us while we were reading. And now it's speeding up."

But the others were no longer listening. Instead they had crowded together to stare out of the window at the blood-red moon swiftly rising over Wizard's Hall.

Just as the moon passed beyond the window's frame, the great bell shattered the library's silence.

"Assembly," Will said, turning around.

"But why should there be an assembly? And at this time of night?" asked Tansy. "I thought the magisters wanted to keep the students out of it."

"Maybe — maybe it wasn't the magisters who rang the bell," Gorse said ominously.

Thornmallow found himself shivering again, this time so hard his top teeth clattered against his lower ones. But when Will grabbed his hand and pulled him out of the room, he dutifully followed, turning left and marching down the hall.

16

THE MASTER AND THE BEAST

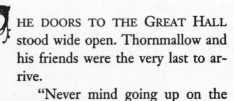HE DOORS TO THE GREAT HALL stood wide open. Thornmallow and his friends were the very last to arrive.

"Never mind going up on the balcony," Gorse said.

"Right." Will slipped in through the doors, turning back to add, "If we're to do anything, we need to be up close."

They pushed through the students in the aisle and made their way forward. Everyone was whispering and the sound of it was like waves in the sea, *see-wash*, *see-wash* over and over. There were no seats left, and so they sat huddled together on the floor in front of the first row.

No one was on the dais yet, but the magisters all stood along the right-hand wall, talking animatedly. Only Magister Hickory was missing.

"Maybe it was Hickory who called the meeting," Thornmallow whispered, remembering the magister's entrance the last time. But the others shook their heads, and even he was unconvinced.

Just then the lights flickered and dimmed, and the great school gong reverberated once again. Instantly, the room grew still.

All eyes turned forward, and Thornmallow could feel tension, thick as new butter, filling the Hall. Magister Hickory stumbled onto the stage from behind a wine-dark curtain. His hair was once again hanging limp against his shoulders and his right hand cradled the left against his chest. Turning his head to stare behind him into the shadows, he looked like a frightened creature being chased through tall grass.

A high chittering broke the vast silence. It took Thornmallow a moment to locate its source. Dr. Mo, raging back and forth and pounding the bars of the cage, was screaming *squark*s so quickly, no one could translate.

Suddenly the lights shot up to full force. A figure cloaked in dark green strode onto the stage, standing behind Magister Hickory. His hair flared out in a black halo around his head and his black beard was braided in a hundred braids. He held the great staff.

"Nettle!" Gorse silently mouthed the name at Thornmallow.

Nettle raised the staff, and at that, even Dr. Mo was mute. Then the black-haired wizard, with casual disdain, pushed Magister Hickory aside with his left hand. Magister Hickory flinched as if he had been badly burned.

Covered with stinging hairs, Thornmallow reminded himself.

"You will call me *Master!*" commanded Nettle, flinging his arms wide.

"Master . . Master . . . Master," came the dutiful response from the students, an avalanche of sound reminding Thornmallow of the snow crashing through the classroom wall. He found he was unable to stop himself and called out the Master's name with the others.

"And you will keep your eyes on me," Nettle continued, waving his left hand languidly toward the rear of the room. "Only me." He giggled, and the sound was surprisingly high-pitched.

They smelled the Beast before they heard it. It was the same smell Thornmallow had encountered in the magister's room: something wet and old and horrible, like a blanket left too long in a damp cellar. And he remembered as well Magister Briar Rose cautioning, "Better not remark any more on it."

Then came the sound, a strange asymmetric lumbering. First it seemed to be coming from somewhere outside; then gathering speed down the hallway; and finally — loud and distinct, yet strangely muffled — right outside the Great Hall doors.

No one turned around to look. No one dared. Compelled by the Master's words and by fear itself, they all stared straight ahead and, as if one body, held their breath.

Something impossibly large stomped down the aisle. It was larger than a dog, larger than a cow, larger even than a wagon loaded high with hay. It was larger than anything Thornmallow could comfortably imagine, but he only glimpsed it out of the corner of his eye.

Slowly and awkwardly the massive creature climbed the stairs, making its way onto the stage. Only then could they see it for what it really was.

It was as tall as the Master at the shoulder, its bulky head towering high above him. There were great swatches of color all over its body, no two alike. Dark lines, like awful scars, ran across its back and shoulders and under its stomach and groin. Each leg was patchworked with the lines. And the lines, running like rivers over its muzzle and under its jaw, seemed to ooze, though whether with sap or blood or tears or infection, Thornmallow could not tell.

Quilted, he thought to himself. *It really is quilted. But I wouldn't want anything like that on my bed.*

The Beast quite suddenly opened its mouth, and its sharp silver teeth glittered. Horribly, it had no tongue.

The Master smiled and let his hand drop, giggling that high giggle again. At once the hall was abuzz with questions. Everybody talked at once. Everybody but Thornmallow. He was silent, trying to remember all he'd read about nettles just an hour before.

Trying.

But for all that he tried, he could not remember a single line.

17

MAGISTER HICKORY'S DEFENSE

AM THE MASTER," SAID THE WIZARD Nettle, "and *this* is the Beast. Do not think to stop us. Do not even try. See what happens to those who would." He pointed down into the room at Register Oakbend and at the cage holding the now silent Dr. Mo.

For the first time Thornmallow saw that the little white creature was not a mouse at all. Or a shrew. Or a vole. Or any other tiny animal. It was a miniature human being dressed in white, its hands waving in agitation.

"Dr. Mo," Thornmallow whispered to himself as if adding up a string of numbers. "*Dr. Mo*-rning Glory. Oh!"

"And there!" said the Master, pointing this time at Magister Hickory, still crouching over his scalded hand.

Thornmallow cried out, "Try, Magister Hickory. Please — *try!*" His voice was too weak to be heard.

Still, Magister Hickory must have heard something, because he nodded to himself, shook himself all over, and slowly stood, his wounded hand red and inflamed before him.

"We have . . . ," Magister Hickory began, flinching once when the Master raised his nettlesome hand. "We have . . . ," he began again, his wavering voice starting to grow stronger, the red hand paling down to a pink, "the number to defeat you, Nettle. We have one hundred and thirteen students. Sing, children! On the dominant!" He sang out a note, and all around Thornmallow the students began to sing the note back. When Thornmallow opened his mouth and tried, he missed the note by at least half a tone. But he *did* try.

The Master laughed, high and hollow. "You have nothing. You never had anything. Numbers are mere fingers on a hand, symbols on a page, nothing. Your casual mathematics mean zero to me, nil, null, nothing. What are one hundred and thirteen children singing? Openmouthed bottles over which wind plays. Nothing."

He held up the staff before him, and the sound the students were making stopped at once. Thornmallow felt the breath sucked out of him, and his note, along with the others, was gone.

"Number . . . ," Magister Hickory tried again. "Number one hundred and thirteen, as it says in the spell." He waved his hands before him, the good hand and the reddened one, which was once again a bright painful color. His fingers made complicated signs in the air. From his fingertips a bit of smoke wavered, wobbled, and at last dissipated into a strange unnatural darkness.

The Master struck the ground with the globe end of the staff. Little lightning cracks darted across the globe's face. At each crack, a similar crack appeared on Magister Hickory's face, until his skin looked like parchment with a map of the Dales written across it. He no longer spoke.

Then the Master lifted the staff, pointing it directly at Magister Hickory, who was still desperately waving his fingers. A thin line of *something* seemed to spin out of Magister Hickory's open mouth. It was as if a thread were being pulled out of the cloth of his being, and he was unraveling before their eyes. The unraveling took a long minute, unwinding the magister into a golden-red thread, then winding him up again around the bulky back of the Beast. When the unraveling and the winding up were done, a new patch had appeared on the Beast's shoulder, a patch as red-gold as the thread, as red-gold as Magister Hickory's hair with the faint imprint of a face on its surface. The Beast belched, and Magister Hickory's empty robe fluttered to the ground.

Thornmallow felt himself sigh, a sound so quiet he doubted anyone near him could hear it. But it felt like a small surrender.

"And now," the Master declared, "oldest to newest, you will do my bidding. You will mount the steps and add to the beauty of my Beast." He smiled horribly. "As your own Magister Hickorystick could do naught against me, not a one of you will be able to do anything more. Best come along quietly and get this done without any messy fight. Remember the words: Punctuality, Practicality, Personality. So come one at a time when I call. It's the only thing you *can* do. After all . . . " He laughed again. "Of the one hundred thirteen students, of the thirteen magisters, whose personality is the dominant one?" He raised his staff high overhead, and all the magisters stood upright as if they were marionettes jerked to their feet by invisible strings. Magister Briar Rose tried to raise her hand and failed.

"Once I was not good enough for the Hall, but now I will quarter my Beast here!" the Master said.

And after Wizard's Hall, Thornmallow thought desperately, *he will take all the Dales*. He wondered briefly what color he would make on the Beast's big body. He wondered what color patch his dear ma would make. He was much too frightened to cry.

18

THE END
OF WIZARD'S HALL

LOWLY THE LINE OF MAGISTERS, compelled beyond any resistance moved across the room to the stairs.

"Try, oh please try," Thornmallow cried in his mind. But he could not get the words out. And what good, he wondered, were one hundred and thirteen students if not one of them could make a sound?

Register Oakbend stumbled forward, his empty hands outstretched before him. Magister Beechvale, like a tamed bird, walked on trembling stork legs. Magister Briar Rose, holding onto the tail of Beechvale's robe, came after. Her cheeks were spotty, as if she had been crying. Pale as paper, Magister Hyssop followed.

In the line of unprotesting magisters came Magisters Greybane and Lilybell, Black Thorn and White Ash and the rest. They climbed step by step without protest, eyes staring at the floor.

Thornmallow named each one to himself as they shuffled across the stage, and he cried silently to each of them to try. Only Magister Briar Rose turned around when he named her. She looked terrified, and her eyes were as blind as Register Oakbend's. Thornmallow was certain she could not see.

One at a time the magisters stood before the Master as, giggling, he raised the staff and pointed the cracked globe toward them. One by one, a deadly arithmetic, they unraveled as the students watched.

Register Oakbend was spun out into an off-white thread, Beechvale a beige, Briar Rose a soft lavender, Hyssop a brilliant yellow. Greybane and Lilybell, Black Thorn and White Ash and the rest were as easily stretched out into thin colored strands, a rainbow of death, the imprint of their faces like a ghastly portrait gallery on the Beast's patchworked hide, while beside the Master the pile of discarded gowns grew.

With each new patch, Thornmallow felt smaller himself, diminished by the losses in a way he could not understand.

Why don't they try? he groaned inside. But he knew the answer. They *had* tried. That was the chance they'd been given. That was the fairness. But what they tried was not nearly enough. The Master was too strong for them — for Magister Hickory, for Register Oakbend, for all of them.

For the first time Thornmallow felt despair.

With a wave of his hand, the Master brought up the fourth-year students. They marched like clockwork dolls in a line. Thornmallow looked away, the only protest he could manage.

If I don't look, he thought, *perhaps it won't be real.*

But he could still hear the drag of feet across the floor, up the stairs, and over the stage. He could still hear the thinning out as, one by one, the students were threaded and patched onto the Beast.

Fourth-years, then third-years, then seconds went without his watching. But when it was the turn of the firsts, he could not help himself. For these were his friends. Thornmallow knew he could not let them go without being their only witness.

He looked up at the stage just as Gorse was winking out, her yellow hair drawn out in a thin gold line.

Oh, Gorse! Thornmallow thought, staring at the Beast where a bright yellow patch with the shadow portrait of Gorse appeared on the right side of the creature's neck.

The Beast was as big now as a barn mow and puffed out with patches. Hardly moving, it seemed somehow horribly content. But still it smelled, if anything — worse than before.

113

Thornmallow's entire body felt cold, too cold to allow for shivering. His tongue cleaved to the roof of his mouth, which kept him from uttering a word. His palms were as wet as if he had just washed them. He would have dried them against his robe if they'd obeyed him. But he couldn't move. He couldn't even blink. Not without the Master's command. All he could do was stare — as one after another of his friends disappeared: three boys he'd sat near in Curses, then Wormwood, as brassy a yellow as his hair, then Will.

Will! But Thornmallow could make no sound except in his head. Will's name echoed there long after his sassy red patch had shown up on the Beast's shoulder, his red freckles dotting the hide.

And then there were but a few students before him, and Thornmallow felt himself jerked upright. As if boneless, he found himself marching toward the stairs. Trying so hard to reach out, past the Master's magic, to touch Tansy's hand for comfort — for she was the fourth student ahead of him — Thornmallow stumbled over his own feet.

The jarring released him for just a moment and he thought: *What about quilts?* Standing up again slowly, he had time for another thought: *Tansy never told us anything she'd learned about them.* And then he realized that in less than a minute he would know rather intimately more about quilts than he ever wanted to know.

114

19

THORNMALLOW
REALLY TRIES

HE CLOSER THORNMALLOW GOT
to the top of the stairs, the more
frightened he became. And the more
frightened he became, the angrier he
got. And the angrier he got, the more
leaden his feet felt, until he was hardly able to drag
one after the other. If he could have, he would have
sunk to his knees and never taken another step again.
But his body kept moving to the Master's command.

When he reached the top step there were only
five students left between him and the patchworked
Beast — three boys, a girl with an orange braid, and
Tansy. Thornmallow thought of a curse. Not a
wizardly curse. A farmer's curse, smudgy but heart-
felt.

"Cow pucker!" he thought. And then he was shocked when the words actually fell aloud from his mouth. Glancing up, he saw that the Master had been at that very moment kicking aside a pile of empty student gowns and smiling to himself. That moment of broken concentration, with the Master so sure of himself that he'd let down his guard, had become a moment of relief. But of the six students left, only Thornmallow seemed to have noticed.

Nettles, Thornmallow thought grimly, *boiled and eaten*. His stomach rumbled, but he couldn't imagine boiling or eating another person. It would have to be something else. *Cut small and granulated*. But he had no knife, nor any mortar or pestle with which to grind the wizard fine. And he couldn't imagine the wizard standing still for any such operation either.

But there was something more about nettles. He thought frantically. Something was missing. *It had to do with names. True Names. Other names.*

Looking up from the gowns, and still smiling, the Master began to focus again on the six remaining students.

Try! Thornmallow urged himself desperately. *Try to remember.*

And then there were only four others ahead of him, and a bright blue patch appeared on the Beast's right rear leg that hadn't been there before.

The Beast shifted its great bulk, and the moonlight through the colored glass window lit two of the patches on its enormous body, a red patch and a white one.

Red, thought Thornmallow suddenly. *And white. That's it!* If he could have smiled at that moment, he would have. *Red Nettle. White Nettle. Those were two of the names. If I can only remember the others . . .* He concentrated even harder and could almost see the book in his mind, his finger on the words. But he concentrated so hard, he tripped over his own feet again, knocking against the boy in front of him. That boy fell against the next boy, who tumbled into the girl with the orange braid, who stumbled into Tansy.

Tansy fell straight forward, her forehead coming to rest against the instep of the Master's shoe. Startled, the Master growled, a sound that filled the room.

Blind Nettle! Thornmallow remembered. His hand grasped the next boy's leg for support as the words spilled out aloud.

As if those words became suddenly real, amplified by the five children linked hand to leg to arm to small of the back to forehead against the instep of a shoe, the thought traveled. It raced across the bridge of bodies and up into the Master's flesh until he screamed. It was an awful scream, high-pitched and full of terror. He put his hands up to his eyes, and when he took them away at last, his eyes were the color of old pearl, gray-white and opaque.

From the side of the room came an answering scream.

Squark! cried Dr. Mo in her cage.

Thornmallow tried to recall the rest of the nettle names. *After Blind Nettle came . . .* He got it!

"False Nettle!" This time he was able to say it aloud easily.

Once again the magic traveled across the span of the children, making the false wizard Nettle writhe in disgust. His wicked deeds multiplied in his mind and he dropped the staff. It clattered to the floor.

"Deaf Nettle!" Thornmallow cried out, not daring to look at the wizard, but certain he could hear Nettle's deafness creeping up on him.

And then Thornmallow sat up, simultaneously letting go his hold on the next boy's leg. He shouted triumphantly, "Dead Nettle!"

Nothing happened.

"Dead Nettle!" Thornmallow cried again, desperation in his voice.

Again nothing happened except that the wizard, now blind and deaf and furious, felt his way up the line of children until he came to Thornmallow.

"You!" he spat, grabbing Thornmallow's arm. "You think you are some kind of hero."

118

Thornmallow trembled in the wizard's grasp.

"You have a magic I do not know. But I will take it from you before I quilt you to the Beast. Give it to me."

"Please, sir," Thornmallow said, painfully aware he was whining, "I am no hero at all. And I have no magic. I am completely tone deaf."

But the Master, blind and deaf, could neither see nor hear his excuse. He grabbed Thornmallow up by the ears, yanking him to his feet.

From somewhere to his right, through the muffling of the wizard's hands, Thornmallow could hear Tansy call out, "Roses in snow, Thorny. Remember — roses in snow."

Thornmallow squeezed his eyes shut until he was as blind as the Master, concentrating on the feel of the wizard's palms over his ears. He remembered what had happened when Magister Beechvale's hands had covered his ears: how the heat had spread from the hands into his ears and down into his brain. But that had been a quiet, comforting heat, and this was red-hot and stinging. Still, when that red-hot stinging heat burrowed into his brain, Thornmallow opened his mouth and a proper magical tone came out. On the dominant.

He began to sing, making up both words and tune as he went, and if it sounded a great deal like a jump-rope rhyme from Hallowdale, that is not surprising:

> Cut the Nettle, grind it small,
> Save the day for Wizard's Hall.
> White and Bee and Hedge and Red,
> Blind and False and Deaf and . . .

he hesitated, drew in a deep breath, and sang out loudly, "DEAD!"

As Thornmallow sang out the last word, he opened his eyes wide, staring into the Master's face, adding, "Rule number five — Magic happens when it's *meant*."

The wizard's pearly eyes stared straight ahead. His ears were deaf. Yet still he could somehow sense the spell. Without speaking another word, and with a look of monstrous surprise on his face, he dropped senseless to the floor. Then, as Thornmallow watched, Nettle disappeared one limb at a time: right leg, left leg, left arm, right arm, the edges fuzzing slightly like trees in a fog. Next his body went, and finally his head. The last to go were the pearly eyes, which suddenly winked out like stars behind passing clouds.

At once the heat in Thornmallow's brain vanished, and the tone in his brain was gone as well, but the stinging on the outside of his ears went on and on and on.

20

UNQUILTING THE BEAST

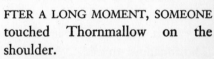FTER A LONG MOMENT, SOMEONE touched Thornmallow on the shoulder.

"Thorny," Tansy asked, "why are you weeping?"

He looked at her, and she seemed all fuzzy at the edges. For a moment he was afraid she was going to disappear like the Master. Then he realized she was fuzzy because there were tears in his eyes, and that is when he *really* started crying. "Because . . . ," he blubbed, "because I should feel like a hero — powerful and strong and victorious and triumphant. Only I feel awful instead. Awful. And unclean. As if I did something wrong."

"You really *are* squishy within," said the orange-haired girl. "And you've got smudges on your nose."

"Nevertheless," one of the boys said, "you killed the wicked wizard."

"And," added the other, "there's nothing at all wrong with that."

Just then the Beast turned its gigantic head and looked mournfully in their direction. It opened its tongueless mouth, and the great silver teeth glittered. But the only sound that came out was "*Moooooooooo.*"

"It's . . . it's just a beast after all," said Tansy.

"A beast of burden," the two boys said together.

"Ghastly burdens," reminded the girl with orange hair.

"So it was the Master who had all the magic," Thornmallow mused. "And not the Beast. With the Master dead, how will we ever get our friends back?"

"Quilts," Tansy said suddenly in a very matter-of-fact voice, "are simply *articles of bed furniture, pieces of scraps stitched together.*" By the way she recited it, Thornmallow knew she was remembering what she had read.

"At home," the girl with the orange braid said, "whenever I was especially naughty, my father sent me to my room to unpick the day's embroidery. It was to teach me patience and obedience." She grinned.

"It didn't work! But it *did* teach me a great deal about *unpicking*."

"And that is . . . ?" Thornmallow asked.

"Find a place to start. A loose thread," said the girl.

Tansy ran over to the Beast and put a hand on its jaw. The Beast stood there impassively. "Whew! He sure does smell."

"So would you if you were made up of over a hundred people," answered Thornmallow. He went to the rump end.

The boys each took a front leg, and the orange-braid girl took the Beast's right side.

Hand over hand they began to search the Beast's patchworked hide. But each thread seemed secure and wet with its continual oozing. They kept it up for almost an hour.

"Nothing!" Tansy said. "We've won, and yet we've lost." She patted the bright square on the Beast's neck that had been Gorse.

"Don't give up yet," Thornmallow said. And as if he heard his own dear ma speaking to him again, he added, "We must try." So saying, he reached as high up on the Beast's rump as he could get, and his hand accidentally brushed the stringy tail. "That's it!" he whispered to himself, grabbing onto the thing. He gave it a great pull as if ringing a church bell.

At the first tug, the tail made a wrenching noise, and the Beast opened its mouth again. But the sound that came out this time was a great ripping noise, like a tent tearing in the wind.

"Wind it up!" shouted the orange-haired girl. "Wind it — never mind, give it to me." And with consummate skill, she began to wind the unraveling threads, thick as good yarn, around her arm and hand.

At each turn of the yarn, a piece of patchwork popped off the Beast's hide, fluttering down to the ground: red patches and blue, turquoise and gold, lavender and umber, sepia and henna, sorrel, copper, apricot, and green. At last the Beast was nothing but a mouth, two eyes, and a sigh.

"What now?" asked Thornmallow.

But none of the others had an answer.

"Squark!"

21

SAVING WIZARD'S HALL

E'VE FORGOTTEN DR. MO," TANSY cried. "She'll know what to do."

The two boys ran down the stairs together and grabbed the cage. They brought it back carefully, setting it gently between the piles of patches and gowns.

"What *should* we do, Dr. Mo?" Tansy asked, kneeling down so she was eye to eye with the tiny wizard.

"*Squark!*"

"She may know what to do," Thornmallow said, "but we can't understand her if all she says is '*squark*'." He opened the cage door and reached in. "But maybe she can show us." Gingerly he picked her up between his thumb and first finger.

"*Squark.*"

Thornmallow let out a gasp and almost dropped her.

"What is it?" the others asked.

"She distinctly said to put her in between the Beast's jaws," he answered.

"She distinctly said '*Squark*,'" said the orange-haired girl.

"And there's no Beast left," added the boys.

"But there *is* a jaw," said Tansy, pointing. "Upper and lower."

Indeed there was: upper and lower floating in the air, along with the mournful eyes and the sharp silver glittering teeth.

"But you can't really mean to put her there," Tansy said. "If the jaws still work, the teeth will chew her to pieces. And if not, the fall from that height will kill her. Are you sure you understand her correctly, Thornmallow?"

"*Squark!*"

Thornmallow's mouth was set in a thin, grim line. "I understand."

"Then you must think, Thornmallow" Tansy said.

"Yes, think!" agreed the others.

Thornmallow thought. "Pile the gowns up as high under the jaws as they will go. And get Magister Hickory's staff. We'll prop the jaws open so the teeth can't close to bite. And we'll cushion her fall with the gowns."

"That's a great solution!" cried Tansy.

126

"But not a magical one," added the orange-haired girl.

Thornmallow smiled shyly. "Maybe not, but I wasn't lying to the wizard. I really *don't* have any magic."

"But you certainly do try hard. And so will we," said Tansy, starting to pile up the gowns beneath the Beast's still-visible jaws. The orange-haired girl helped her.

It took both boys to carry the heavy staff, and then they had to stand one atop the other in order to jam the staff in place between the teeth. But after a moment of teetering and another moment of tottering, they were done.

"Now," the boy on top called out, "give me Dr. Mo."

Carefully, Thornmallow handed up the tiny wizard.

"*Squark*," complained Dr. Mo as she was passed from hand to hand.

Thornmallow put his right hand on the lower boy's right shoulder, his left hand on the left shoulder, and sang — not at all well but at least on the dominant:

> Through the jaw and over the teeth,
> Straight on to the gowns beneath,
> From such greatness she will fall,
> Through the Beast, returns to all.

"Let her go!" Thornmallow shouted.

The boy dropped Dr. Mo straight through the

Beast's gaping jaws. The jaws, in mindless reflex, chomped down on Magister Hickory's staff, breaking it in two.

As the two pieces of the staff clattered to the ground, a mighty wind blew up, guttering all the torches in the room, and in the dark came screams of a hundred voices.

"Relight those torches," came one voice overriding the screams, a voice that was both sweet and commanding. "Wizard's Hall must blaze with light. You will find candles in the hallways."

Thornmallow scrambled down the pitch-black stairs and up the darkened aisle, feeling his way until he came to the door. When he swung it open, the hallway candles were a welcome sight, glowing in their sconces. He grabbed up two and ran back, lighting torches along the way.

When all the torches were lit, Thornmallow could see that the stage was crowded with students and magisters, hugging one another, weeping, and sorting through the scholastic robes.

Will stepped to the front of the stage, and Gorse was beside him. They began to wave madly. "Thorny — here. We're all right! You've done it."

And Gorse added, her voice cracking with emotion, "You've saved Wizard's Hall."

22

THE ENHANCER

ITHIN MINUTES THE STUDENTS were back in their seats, stomping and whistling and clapping until their hands hurt. The magisters let them celebrate, and even Magister Beechvale found himself tapping his foot in rhythm to the applause.

But at last the cheers began to subside, and Magister Hickory strode up to the stage, his hair standing about his head like a red-gold lion's mane. A tall woman greeted him. She was dressed in flowing white robes, and her dark hair cascaded down either side of a heart-shaped face.

Thornmallow recognized her at once: Magister Dr. Morning Glory. Dr. Mo.

Magister Hickory picked up one end of the shattered staff, and Dr. Morning Glory picked up the other. When they placed the two halves together, the entire assembly arose and began cheering madly again. But the cheering stopped when it was clear that the two halves were not sticking together.

Dr. Morning Glory raised her hand, and the room was immediately still. "Young Thornswallow, you who saved Wizard's Hall," she called out. "Come up here to us."

Shyly, Thornmallow stood. He had to push his way through several of his friends before marching proudly up the stairs. This time he didn't stumble. All the while, the students below the stage were calling, "Thorn-ny! Thorn-ny! Thorn-ny!"

When he reached the top step, Dr. Morning Glory held her hand up again for silence, then once more placed her end of the staff against Magister Hickory's.

"Now, my boy," she said, her voice as lilting as a song, "come and put your hands on top of the stick, but do not touch our hands."

Thornmallow did as he was told, and all at once a glow encased the staff, moving up and down the stick, healing the break even as they watched.

"Now, child, take your hands away," whispered Dr. Morning Glory.

He did — and was amazed. The staff held together.

Dr. Morning Glory raised the staff above her head so that all the hall might see.

"That's wandy!" cried out a third-year student, and they all clapped.

"I don't understand," Thornmallow mumbled. "Do I have a talent for magic — or don't I?"

She smiled at him but then looked past him and spoke to the entire room. "Thornpower asks if he has a talent for magic." She smiled slowly and shook her head. "He does not. At least, he does not have a talent for *enchantment*. His talent is far greater. He has a talent for *enhancement*. He can make any spell someone else works even greater simply by trying."

Slowly Dr. Morning Glory lowered the staff and handed it to Magister Hickory. "Alone he is only an ordinary boy, the kind who makes our farms run and our roads smooth, who builds our houses and fights our wars. But when he touches wizards he trusts and admires — or their staffs — he makes their good magicks better. When he touches wizards he hates and fears, he turns their own evil magicks against them."

She turned and spoke to Magister Hickory, but her voice had such power, everyone could hear her. "We magisters — in our pride — thought we understood the dark magic that was at work. We were given the rhyme by Nettle:

> Ever on the quilting goes,
> Spinning out the lives between,
> Winding up the souls of those
> Students up to one-thirteen.

And we read it thinking we needed one hundred and thirteen students here at the Hall. But we didn't need all one hundred and thirteen. We needed just the one. The final one. The enhancer. The one who would really *really* try."

There was a sudden whispering throughout the room, and Dr. Morning Glory let it go on for a while before silencing it.

"My fellow wizards," she began again. "My dear students, my colleagues, my friends: every community needs its enhancers. Even more than it needs its enchanters. They are the ones who appreciate us and understand us and even save us from ourselves."

She put her hands on Thornmallow's shoulder, and all at once he could feel the stinging in his ears again.

As if she felt the pain herself, Dr. Morning Glory leaned over so that her mouth was close to his left ear. "You will always have that pain, child," she whispered, "whenever a wizard touches you. The stinging nettle hairs are embedded deep. But the pain will remind you of your strength, of what you have done, of what you *can* do — if you truly try."

He looked over his shoulder at her, and it was suddenly as if he were staring at his own dear ma.

"Can I stay?" he asked. "Here at Wizard's Hall? Even if I am not an enchanter?"

"It may often be painful."

"I don't care about that."

She smiled and pulled a white handkerchief embroidered with the letters *MG* from the air. Carefully, gently, she rubbed a spot on his nose. "Of course you can stay. We couldn't do without you, Thornbarrow."

"Thornmallow," he said. Then he looked back at the cheering crowd. Ears burning, he waved his hands triumphantly, feeling nicely prickly on the outside and — if truth be known — fairly squishy within.

Let your imagination fly with the best in fantasy

MAGIC CARPET BOOKS

DIANE DUANE's thrilling wizardry series

So You Want to Be a Wizard (0-15-201239-7) $6.50
Fleeing a bully, Nita discovers a manual on wizardry in her library. But magic
doesn't solve her problems—in fact, they've only just begun!

Deep Wizardry (0-15-201240-0) $6.00
The novice wizards join a group of dolphins, whales, and one giant shark in an
ancient magical ritual—a ritual that must end with a bloody sacrifice.

High Wizardry (0-15-201241-9) $6.00
Nita and Kit face their most terrifying challenge yet: Nita's bratty little sister,
Dairine—the newest wizard in the neighborhood!

A Wizard Abroad (0-15-201207-9) $6.00
Nita's Irish vacation from magic turns out to be the opposite! Ireland is even more
steeped in wizardly dangers than the States. So much for a vacation abroad. . . .

The first book in EDITH PATTOU's epic Songs of Eirren

Hero's Song (0-15-201636-8) $6.00
The trail of his sister's kidnappers leads Collun to a giant white wurme whose
slime is acid to the touch, a wurme that Collun must kill if he is to rescue his
sister and save his world.

MEREDITH ANN PIERCE's classic Darkangel Trilogy

The Darkangel (0-15-201768-2) $6.00
Aeriel must kill the wicked Darkangel before he finds his fourteenth bride—even
though within him is a spark of goodness that could redeem even *his* evil.

Let your imagination fly

... by joining the Magic Carpet Book Club!

Buy any three Magic Carpet books, and get a free fantasy novel!

Getting your free fantasy novel is easy. Just buy three Magic Carpet books and clip the proof of purchase tab from the corner of each book club page. (If the Magic Carpet books you buy do not have a book club page, send in your register receipts listing each title purchased as proof of purchase.) Then fill out the order form below and send it, along with proof of all three purchases, to:

Magic Carpet Book Club
Harcourt Brace & Company
525 B Street, Suite 1900
San Diego, CA 92101

And we'll send you a free book!